Shadows on Society Hill

An Addy Mystery

by Evelyn Coleman

★ Ameri

Published by American Girl Publishing
Copyright © 2007, 2015 American Girl

Questions or comments? Call 1-800-845-0005,
visit **americangirl.com**, or write to Customer Service,
American Girl, 8400 Fairway Place, Middleton, WI 53562.

Printed in China
15 16 17 18 19 20 21 LEO 10 9 8 7 6 5 4 3 2 1

Cover image by Juliana Kolesova

The following individuals and organizations have given permission to
use images incorporated into the cover design: Society Hill row houses, used
by permission of Ron Saari; iron fence, Ana Vasileva/Shutterstock.com; mine,
Neil Lockhart/Shutterstock.com; ladder, sirikorn thamniyon/Shutterstock.com;
background pattern on back cover, © kirstypargeter/Crestock.

Cataloging-in-Publication Data available from the Library of Congress

To my daughter Latrayan (Sankofa) Mueed,
who pushed me through this process.

To Peg Ross, you are the editor authors dream
would appear. How happy I am you're in my life.

Beforever™

The adventurous characters you'll meet in
the BeForever books will spark your curiosity
about the past, inspire you to find your voice
in the present, and excite you about your future.
You'll make friends with these girls as you share
their fun and their challenges. Like you, they are
bright and brave, imaginative and energetic,
creative and kind. Just as you are, they are
discovering what really matters: Helping others.
Being a true friend. Protecting the earth.
Standing up for what's right. Read their stories,
explore their worlds, join their adventures.
Your friendship with them will BeForever.

TABLE *of* CONTENTS

chapter 1

A Daring Rescue

ADDY SPOTTED THE man crossing the street only seconds before she saw the large brown horse break away from the carriage. The man continued walking, his heavy boots making prints in the snow. Addy shouted, "Mister, get out of the way!"

The man evidently didn't hear the thunderous hooves of the horse, or the screams of several women. Addy sprinted toward him and at the same time called out, "Poppa, help!"

Addy's poppa was on a ladder in front of a nearby building. He was repairing the overhang. "Addy, what's wrong?" Poppa shouted. He practically flew down the ladder, knocking over a bucket of nails as he jumped, missing six rungs.

Addy's heartbeat pounded in her ears as she dove for the man, knocking him to the ground.

The horse zoomed past, so close that Addy could feel the ground underneath her shake.

"Addy! Addy! Are you hurt?" Poppa asked, grabbing her up into his arms and hugging her close. "What happened?"

The man brushed snow from his heavy fur coat as he got up. "She saved my life, that's what happened," the man said, unwrapping his black scarf from his face.

A few people stood around mumbling. A white woman said, "That colored girl just knocked that man down."

"The horse broke loose, Poppa, when the carter was trying to fix his bridle," Addy said quickly, defending her actions. "I didn't mean to knock the man down."

"Of course she didn't. She was trying to save me," the man said, frowning at the woman. "Go on now. The show is over," he said to the small crowd gathered round.

As the people wandered off, the man turned back to Addy and Poppa. "I had these in my ears," the man said, holding up two wads of cotton. "The cold weather irritates my eardrums. I didn't even realize the horse was coming toward me. Thank you, young lady. Let me shake your hand."

"You sure you all right?" Poppa asked Addy. He still held her tight, his face riddled with concern.

Addy felt a little shaky, but she answered in a confident voice, "Yes, Poppa, I'm sure."

Poppa put Addy down. But he held on to her shoulder. Addy's fingers were frozen stiff, but she stuck out her hand to the man.

"Why, you're just a little girl," he said.

"I'm eleven years old," Addy replied. Her hand was so cold that even the shake hurt.

Poppa said, "I'm glad you ain't hurt, sir." He turned to walk away.

"Wait," said the man, fumbling inside his coat. "I'd like to give your daughter a reward for saving my life."

Addy looked at Poppa. But before he could speak, she said, "No thank you, sir."

Poppa smiled down at her.

"But I . . ." the man said, holding out a ten-dollar bill.

Addy stared at the money. Ten dollars would pay for a whole year of schooling at the Institute for Colored Youth. She wanted to take it. They needed the money. Poppa hadn't had steady work for going on four months. But Addy could see on Poppa's face that he wouldn't like it if she took it. "It's fine, sir," she said. "I was just doing what any decent person would do."

"But . . ." the man said.

"We fine, sir," Poppa said, walking back to the ladder. "I'm glad you are not hurt either, sir. Addy, let me grab my tools and we can go on home. Your momma needs to make sure you didn't hurt your-self none." Poppa climbed up on the ladder, this time skipping every other step.

The man eyed the overhang that Poppa had been repairing and then asked, "Did you do that fancy woodwork up there?"

"Yes, sir, I did," Poppa said, snatching his hammer from the overhang.

"Where did you learn to do such elaborate woodworking?" the man asked.

"I learned some working on fancy summer houses on Cape Island, New Jersey," Poppa said. "Taught myself the rest."

The man pointed to the sign just below the overhang, *Milner's Builders.* "Do you work for this company?"

"No, sir. The owner just let me take this little job to show him what I can do. He says he ain't got no other work right now, but if I do a good job, he might well call me back soon."

"Would you like to come work for me?"

Addy watched Poppa's face excitedly. A job. Poppa wanted a job. Just this morning, he'd said he'd do any kind of work. Addy hoped Poppa would take the job the man had to offer. But she also hoped that it wouldn't take Poppa away again. Last summer when Poppa worked in New Jersey, Addy sure had missed him.

Poppa said, "Well, I sure need a job, sir. I can do 'most any kind of carpentry. I can read and write, too. And Mr. Miles Roberts will tell you I'm a good worker."

"That," the man said, pointing to the overhang, "is all the reference you need. I'd pay you a fair wage. I have men working on my houses right now, but none of them can do this type of work. I would love to have you do some of this fancy woodworking for me. Let me introduce myself. I'm Albert Radisson. I'm an architect."

The man lifted his gloved hand to his face.

He removed the glove with his teeth and stuck out his hand.

Poppa wiped his hand on his overalls and shook Mr. Radisson's hand. "Sir, thank you. I won't let you down," Poppa said. "When do you want me to start?"

Poppa kept shaking the man's hand. Addy thought, *As cold as it is out here, if Poppa shakes that man's hand any harder, it might break off.*

Finally the man pulled his hand back. He searched in his coat. "Here is my address," he said, scribbling on a piece of paper. "I'll expect you Monday morning—early."

Poppa took Addy's hand as the man walked away. "Did you hear that, Addy? I have a new job, thanks to you," he said. "I'm sure glad you wanted to spend your Saturday with me. What a stroke of luck." Poppa quickly gathered up his tools and supplies. He smiled at Addy as they turned and hurried toward the boarding house.

Addy smiled back. This was going to be the best year ever. The war was over and now all the slaves were free. Addy was doing well at the Institute for Colored Youth. Sam, her brother, and Esther, her little sister, were here with the family in Philadelphia now.

Yes, 1866 was turning out just like Addy had dreamed of when she and Momma escaped slavery.

chapter 2
Snowfall

ON MONDAY AFTERNOON, Addy hurried home from school in a light snowfall. As she walked, she tried to catch snowflakes on her tongue. Snow reminded Addy how easily "good" disappeared. One day, snow falls from the sky as white and fluffy as cotton; then, when the sun pops out, it melts away and it's gone. That's how life was.

Now Addy understood Auntie Lula's saying, *If it ain't one thing, it's another.* How else could you explain: The minute Poppa finds a new job, the woman Momma works for, Mrs. Ford, announces she's moving to Maine with her sister and closing the dress shop.

If only Auntie Lula and Uncle Solomon were

still alive, Addy thought, she could talk to them about all the changes taking place. Addy missed them both. Uncle Solomon and Auntie Lula had helped Addy and her momma escape the plantation. They had also taken care of Addy's baby sister, Esther, after Momma and Addy escaped. It was so sad that Uncle Solomon had died before he and Auntie Lula had reached Philadelphia, bringing Esther to the family. But, as Auntie Lula said, at least Uncle Solomon didn't die still a slave. That was enough for him.

As Addy neared the boarding house, she spotted Poppa through a haze of snowflakes. He was standing at the window of their room, talking to Momma. What was Poppa doing home so early? Had Mr. Radisson let Poppa go already?

The minute Addy walked into the room, she could see that Momma was crying.

"Momma, Poppa," Addy said, "is everything all right?"

Momma pulled Addy to her and cried into Addy's shoulder. Addy hugged her back. She had not seen Momma cry since they ran from North Carolina. "I'm fine, Addy," Momma mumbled through her tears. "Tell her, Ben."

Poppa sat down at the table. "We're moving, Addy."

Addy looked over at Poppa, while Momma dried her tears on the corner of her apron. "Mr. Radisson didn't give you the job like he promised, Poppa?" Addy asked. She felt even more confused when Momma and Poppa both began to smile like somebody just got a molasses cake.

"No, Addy, he did give it to me. Mr. Radisson gonna have plenty of work for me. He's fixing his house up 'cause he's getting married, and he wants things ready before his mother and his fiancée arrive. But, Addy, the best part is, he's done invited us to live in the servants' house in back of his place."

"Really, Poppa?" Addy said, jumping up. "Is it nice?"

"It's the finest place we ever had, Addy. It's right behind his house—right on the edge of Society Hill."

"What?" Momma said, almost choking. "Where the rich people live?"

"That's right," Poppa said. "We are moving to a fine place on Society Hill. Mr. Radisson's uncle left him the house when he died. Mr. Radisson had closed the house up and let his uncle's servants go. The servants were a married couple who had two girls, just like we got. So the house they lived in is all set up. Just needs a little dusting. And, Addy, you and Esther gonna have a room all to yourselves."

"You playing with me, Poppa?" Addy asked. She picked Esther up and swung her around. "Esther, do you hear that?" Addy sang. "We gonna have our own room."

"Hurray!" Esther shouted.

Addy's older brother, Sam, walked in, shaking snow off his coat. "What's going on?"

"Let me riddle him, Poppa," Addy said.

"Okay, riddle away." Poppa smiled at her. "It's 'cause of you, Addy, that it's happened."

"What's happened?" Sam asked, waving his hand for someone to hurry up and tell him something.

"What's big and pretty, and only two girls gonna be in it?" Addy riddled.

"A swing?" Sam guessed.

Addy shook her head.

"A fancy carriage?"

"Nope," Addy said, grinning.

Momma said, "Enough, Addy. Tell him."

"We're moving," Addy said. "To Society Hill. And Esther and I gonna have a room all to ourselves."

Sam looked at Poppa. "You all joking, right?" he asked.

"She's telling the truth, son," Poppa said, quickly filling Sam in. "You gonna have your own room up in the garret, too."

Sam said, "I can't believe it, Poppa."

Addy and Esther danced around, holding hands in a circle, for what seemed like hours. Momma and Poppa laughed and laughed watching the two of them. Sam even joined in after a while. "Come on, Momma and Poppa!" Esther shouted. Addy could not believe it when Momma and Poppa grabbed their hands, too.

The following Sunday evening, a light snow was falling again as Addy and her family gathered at the boarding-house door to say their good-byes to the Goldens.

M'dear, Mr. Golden's mother, hugged Addy close and whispered, "Remember, you are always loved." Addy knew that just because M'dear was blind and couldn't see her tears, that didn't mean she didn't know how much Addy would miss her and Mr. and Mrs. Golden. They were like family. Addy would miss the boarding house too, even though her parents, Sam, Esther, and Addy had all stayed in one room.

Sam glanced out into the chilly dusk. "Good thing we don't have much to move. The snow is picking up outside."

With one last round of hugs and good-byes, the Walkers closed the boarding-house door for the last time. All their belongings were gathered outside, ready to be moved.

They would have to walk to Society Hill. Since Poppa no longer worked for Miles Roberts, he didn't have the use of Mr. Roberts's wagon anymore.

Momma lit the kerosene lamp and said, "Addy, I'm going to let you carry our gift from Mrs. Ford."

Addy took the lamp carefully from Momma's hands. Mrs. Ford had given them the lamp when Addy and Momma lived in the garret over Mrs. Ford's sewing shop. Until that Christmas, a candle had been their only light. It had been hard for Addy to do her assignments for school, and Momma couldn't see well to sew at night. That one lamp had made a world of difference. Addy wondered if this one lamp would be enough light for them in their new home.

Poppa had rigged a trunk with wheels. Now he put the beautiful sled he'd made for Addy and Esther on top, picked up the trunk's rope pull, and slung a sack with the rest of their belongings over his shoulder. Momma carried her sewing supplies wrapped in two huge shawls, and her fabrics in a basket atop her head. Sam lifted Esther up and settled her on his arm. Esther carried her doll, Janie. And Addy carried the lamp, which cast a golden circle of light against the falling snow.

As they walked through the chilly evening, Addy ignored the pain that soon crept into her hands and feet. She didn't care that the snow pelting her face felt sharp as pine needles. Living in Society Hill would be different for her and her family. Her heart was filled with hope as they made their way past the row houses, the alleys, the covered marketplaces, to the area known as Society Hill.

Addy had delivered dresses in Society Hill for Mrs. Ford. She had always admired all the fancy houses. M'dear had told Addy that when she was younger, she had worked on Society Hill as a chore girl. Addy couldn't believe that she was actually going to live in such a fine place as Society Hill. This wasn't even a dream come true, Addy told herself, because she would not ever have dreamed it. Addy couldn't wait to see her new home.

There weren't many people out. Poppa led the way, clearing a path with the rope-rigged trunk so that it was easier for Momma, Sam holding Esther, and Addy to walk on the snow-laden sidewalk.

Addy noticed that the closer they got to Society Hill, the cleaner everything appeared. The bricks of the houses were brighter. There was no trash on the main streets, and even the dark alleys seemed neater. The streetlights looked fancier. Signs on stores were more elaborate, and store windows held all kinds of treats. Addy couldn't help stopping to look into one of the storefront windows.

Sam called to her, "Come on, Addy, catch up now, and stay beside me."

Addy heard her brother, but she was busy admiring a beautiful blue dress with flowers on it. She was about to tear herself away and catch up with her family when she heard a gruff voice behind her shouting, "Stop there, all of you. Not another step!"

Addy turned to find a policeman glaring into

her face. Her heart raced. She had heard plenty of stories in the boarding house about how lots of the police in Philadelphia had belonged to gangs and liked to beat up Irish and colored people.

Poppa hurried to Addy, ignoring the officer's command not to take another step. He stood between the policeman and Addy. Sam too had moved closer to Addy, still carrying Esther on his arm. Momma stood beside Sam.

"Sir, we are on our way to our new home," Poppa said, extending his hand to shake.

The policeman glared at Poppa's hand as if it might be a poisonous water moccasin. "Where did you get all this stuff?" the policeman said, still sounding angry.

"Sir, these are our belongings. We're only a few blocks from our new place."

Sam said, "We don't have a wagon, so we have to walk."

The policeman pointed at Sam. "I ain't speaking

to you, boy." Then he looked directly at Poppa. "Why are you here in Society Hill, is what I'm asking."

"Sir, our home is—"

The policeman held up his hand to silence Poppa. "You want me to believe you're just strolling through Society Hill in a blizzard? Did you steal these things? What about that sled? Looks like it cost a lot of money."

Poppa moved to reach into his pocket. The policeman whacked Poppa's hand so quick and hard, Addy jumped.

Sam tried to hand Esther to Addy. Momma held fast to Sam's arm and shook her head. Sam looked down into the thickening snow.

Poppa acted as though the policeman might just have tried to save him from a mosquito by swatting it away. He pulled from his pocket the slip of paper that had their exact address on it and with a steady hand held it out for the policeman.

"What's it say?" the policeman demanded. "Or can't you read?"

Poppa lifted the paper, dusted off a few flakes of snow, and read the address of their new home, adding, "I am working for Mr. Albert Radisson."

The policeman said, "Ain't no Albert Radisson 'round here."

Quietly Poppa replied, "It's the house Mr. Radisson's uncle left to him, where we going."

The policeman narrowed his eyes. "I'm gonna let you go for now, but I'm coming 'round to check on you when the weather breaks. You better not be lying to me, boy," he said.

"Yes, sir," Poppa answered.

After the policeman had walked away, Poppa said, "Come on. Let's hurry out of this snow. We only have a few more blocks to go," as if nothing had happened.

Addy felt a burning in her nose. She reached up to see if she was bleeding, but she wasn't. She trembled all over. Addy walked next to Sam, hold-ing on to the sleeve that should have covered the arm he'd lost fighting for his country.

She could feel a tear slipping down her face. She did not care that the snow stung her cheeks, or that her toes burned from the frostbite setting in through her shoes, or that her hands could no longer feel the lantern. The excitement she'd felt only an hour ago had melted away like a snowflake on her tongue. Addy's heart hurt.

chapter 3
Uncle Solomon's Protection

ONCE THEY MADE it to Mr. Radisson's, Addy and her family stared up at the three-story brick house. Addy thought it seemed almost as large as her school. She had never seen a house with so many windows. This evening, all the windows were dark. Mr. Radisson had gone to pick up his mother from her home in Virginia and wouldn't be back for a day or two.

Poppa said, "Our house is 'round back."

Addy, Sam, Momma, and Esther followed Poppa around the side of Mr. Radisson's house to the alley, where a wrought-iron gate led into the backyard. Only Esther ran gleefully through the gate. Everyone else paused, just to look at their new home.

Addy saw that there was a smaller house and a shed behind Mr. Radisson's house, each building separated from the others by a patch of yard. Poppa pointed to the smaller house. Like Mr. Radisson's house, it was made of red brick. The two houses were much alike, except that Mr. Radisson's house was much bigger and had a shuttered porch on the back. Trellises lined the porch, twined with wisteria vines. The snow-covered vines looked like a lace tablecloth. Addy wondered if Poppa could plant fancy vines on their house someday.

When Addy and her family walked into the little house, they just hugged each other. It didn't seem real to Addy that they would actually be living in a place so lovely.

The house had a kitchen and a cozy sitting parlor on the first floor. In the kitchen, Addy ran her fingers around the rim of a gas lamp attached directly to the wall. On their old plantation, Master Stevens had had only one gas lamp,

in the parlor. Candles and kerosene lanterns lit the
rest of the house. Addy wondered what Master
Stevens would say if he knew that her family had
gas lamps now.

Racing upstairs, Addy found two bedrooms
on the second floor and a garret up under the roof.
All through the house, the floors were shiny hard-
wood, and the furniture was even better than
Mrs. Ford's furniture. Everything was beautiful.
There was even a little privy on the back of the
house, so they no longer would have to share one
with their neighbors in an alley.

While Poppa helped Momma unpack, Addy
and Esther dusted. Sam worked to get fires burning
in the fireplaces.

Later, Momma cooked cornbread and beans for
supper on the iron stove in the kitchen. They all ate
quietly, taking in the new smells of their first real
home out of slavery. No one brought up what had
happened earlier with the policeman. But Addy

could see that, with the exception of Esther, all of them had it on their hearts, if not their minds.

As Addy helped Esther get ready for bed, she wondered about the family who had lived in the house before. Where were they now? She hoped they had moved to an even prettier place. Addy was about to say that to Esther, but the girl must have gone to sleep the second her head hit the pillow.

Addy was pulling out a schoolbook to read when Sam came to the door. "You sure were quiet tonight," he said. "Are you all right?"

Addy said, "I'm all right."

Sam sat beside her on the edge of her bed. "It's because of you, Addy, and your bravery, that we're here in this nice house," he said, smiling. "And now Poppa has steady work. Thanks to you, things are all changing for the good. You should be really happy, little sister."

Addy looked down at her hands. She wanted to feel happy, but the image of the policeman pushed at her thoughts.

"You can't hide that sadness from me," Sam said. "You thinking 'bout what happened on the way over here tonight?"

Sam always knew when something was bothering her. Addy asked, "Sam, you think white people gonna always be mean to us?"

"Well, not all white people are mean to us. But, truth is, I expect there's always gonna be mean people."

Addy nodded.

"Don't think about it, Addy."

Addy couldn't help it. She didn't want to think about it. But the truth was, she had been so frightened. "I was so scared he was going to hurt you or Poppa," Addy said. "Sometimes I wish we could just be like everyone else."

Sam smiled. "Addy, we are just like everyone

else. Some folks just don't accept that. Maybe some-day everyone will understand how silly it is to think we're any different from anyone else."

Addy lowered her eyes. She didn't want Sam to see that tears had popped into her eyes.

"You know what, Addy? I got something for you," Sam said.

"What is it?" Addy asked.

Sam replied with a riddle. "What's smooth and has an eye on it, and yet can't see?"

Addy smiled despite her sadness. Sam could always cheer her up with a riddle. *Hmm,* Addy thought. "I know. Black-eyed peas."

Sam laughed. "You sure are good at riddling. But that's not what I was talking about. Here, it's right here," Sam said, holding up the leather cord around his neck. A black stone dangled from it.

Addy couldn't believe it. "The protection stone? Sam, are you still riddling me?"

"No, Addy. I think you should have it."

"But Uncle Solomon gave it to you after you saved that little boy from drowning," Addy protested. "And what about you? Don't you need protection?"

Sam held up his one arm. "I've got this. I fought and now there's no more slavery. That's all the protection I need. You saved Mr. Radisson's life. If Uncle Solomon was here, I bet he'd want you to have the stone now."

Sam lifted the necklace from his neck.

Addy always marveled at how well Sam could do things with only one arm. Sometimes she forgot that he'd given his arm for their freedom. Addy smiled. She took the smooth black protection stone into her hands. She could feel tiny bumps pop up on her arms. She gave Sam a hug. "Thank you."

Sam stood up. "You welcome, little sister," he said. "Now you don't have to worry about that policeman or anyone else."

Sam helped Addy put the stone onto her

necklace, where she wore the cowrie shell from her grandmother Aduke. Now she had something from her grandmother and something from Sam and Uncle Solomon around her neck.

Addy said her prayers and Momma tucked her into her feather bed. Addy's body sank into the bed, and the feathers molded up around her, just like the bed was giving her a hug. Addy had never had such a comfortable bed before. She loved her new room.

Addy watched Momma go over and kiss Esther's forehead. Then Momma turned back to Addy. "Sleep tight. Don't let the bedbugs bite."

Addy couldn't help giggling despite her sadness. There used to be bedbugs back at the plantation, but here there were no bedbugs. Addy said, "Good night, Momma," as she watched Momma put out the gas lamp.

The moon cast a sheer light into the bedroom. Addy was glad that her bed was next to the window. Addy glanced over at her little sister's bed. Esther was hugging her doll, Janie. The doll had once been Addy's. Now Addy had Ida Bean, but she'd packed her away in the trunk when she turned eleven.

Esther didn't remember much about their old life. Addy was glad of that. She turned over and snuggled into her pillow. She was having a life she couldn't have even dreamed of while working in the fields all day, her fingers bleeding from picking cotton.

Suddenly, one of Addy's worst memories popped into her mind. Just before she and Momma ran for freedom, the overseer had made Addy eat worms as a punishment because she'd left a few of them still clinging to the tobacco leaves. That day was terrible. Addy would never forget how awful it felt. But then, only a few days later, she and Momma had made their escape. Maybe Auntie Lula was right. *No matter how bad it seem,* she used to say, *don't mean it can't get no better.*

Addy lifted her head to take one more look at her beautiful room. That was when she saw it— a reflection in the mirror over the small dresser. Addy focused on the mirror. There it was again— a flash of light. Addy threw the covers back, knelt on her bed by the window, and peered outside.

She didn't see anything out of place in Mr. Radisson's backyard. The snow had finally stopped, and now the moonlight sparkled on the snowy yard. Everything looked white and fluffy, as if summer clouds had settled on the ground.

Addy was just about to lie back down when another flash of light caught her eye. She blinked. Were the night and the snow playing tricks on her eyes?

She leaned closer to the window. Wait, there it was again—a light moving inside Mr. Radisson's house.

Addy leaned so close to the window that her breath fogged the glass. She used her elbow to clear the windowpane. Was someone inside Mr. Radisson's house? Her heartbeat speeded up. The beats sounded so loud, Addy hoped that they wouldn't wake Esther.

She saw the light again. It moved forward, more steadily now, out onto the porch. Addy clutched her covers as the light shimmered through the trellised vines.

Addy was holding the covers so tight, she could feel her nails digging into her palm. She hunched down and waited. The light flickered wildly. Addy tried not to blink. It seemed as if the light was sinking. Then, suddenly, it was just gone.

Addy felt her entire body trembling. What had she seen? Should she tell Poppa? She felt a chill run down her spine. The light must have been either her imagination or—she didn't want to think it, but it popped into her head anyway—*or a ghost.* On the plantation, people were always talking about seeing ghosts. But Addy hadn't ever seen one. And Momma and Poppa had never said they'd seen one. Addy didn't even believe in ghosts. Did she?

Addy scrambled back down onto the feather bed, snuggled as deep as she could, and put the pillow over her head. She clutched the smooth protection stone in her palm.

It couldn't have been a ghost. It just couldn't.

chapter 4

Troubling Answers

AS SOON AS the first rays of sunlight filtered through the curtains, Addy was wide-awake. She decided to get up early so that she could talk to Poppa. Downstairs, she could hear him moving quietly in the kitchen.

Careful not to disturb Esther or Momma, Addy slipped out of bed and down the stairs. When she reached the kitchen, Poppa was just heading out the door with his lunch pail in his hand.

"Poppa," Addy called.

"Addy, what you doing up so early?"

"I wanted to tell you to have a good day at work."

"Thank you, Addy. I join Mr. Radisson's regular crew today. I'm a little nervous."

"You'll do fine, Poppa," Addy said.

"Thanks. Now go on back to sleep. Before you know it, it'll be time for school."

Addy cleared her throat. "Is Mr. Radisson back, Poppa?"

"No, he'll be making it back tomorrow or the next day with his mother. Why?"

"I thought I saw a light in his house last night," Addy said, trying not to sound frightened.

"Must have been a reflection of the moon or something," Poppa said. He patted Addy on the shoulder. "Ain't nobody 'round that house."

Addy didn't want to argue with Poppa.

"I've gotta hurry, Addy. I can't be late."

"Okay, Poppa," Addy said. "Just one more question."

"Go on, ask it, but hurry."

"Did Mr. Radisson's uncle die in that house?"

"I'm pretty sure he did. Why?"

"Nothing," Addy said. "Nothing."

Poppa gave Addy a kiss on her forehead. "You

have a good day at school," he said. Then he hurried out the door and bounded up the path.

Addy waved to him as he went out the gate. She couldn't remember seeing Poppa so happy. She wouldn't spoil his day with silly talk of ghosts.

That evening, Addy waited for Poppa to come home. She'd decided to ask him if he believed in ghosts. But she swallowed the question when she saw his face. He looked awfully sad.

At dinner Poppa told them what the trouble was. He had shown up for work at least twenty minutes early. When the other four men showed up, none of them even spoke to Poppa. They just went about their work as if they didn't see him. Finally Poppa heard one of them say, "Here comes the boss." Poppa hurried to meet Mr. Gunter. Mr. Radisson had already talked to Mr. Gunter about Poppa's new job.

Poppa said, "He took one look at me and said, 'Sorry, but we don't have no work for you.'"

Addy put down her fork. Her stomach tied into knots.

"At first, I thought he just didn't know who I was. So I introduced myself again, saying that Mr. Radisson sent me. He said, 'Look, I ain't had a chance to tell Radisson, but my men won't work with you. They have threatened to quit if you work. We gotta finish this job this week. So, I'm sorry, but you can't work.'"

"Then what am I supposed to do?" Poppa had asked him. "Mr. Radisson sent me here."

"I tell you what I'll do for you. You can get us water, fetch our tools. Then you can take up your pay with Radisson."

Momma asked, "So what did you do?"

Poppa put some mashed potatoes on his fork. "I helped out."

No one said anything else about it.

Addy wanted to ask Poppa why he didn't just come on back home and wait for Mr. Radisson, but she didn't. She didn't have to ask. Deep down, she knew. Poppa would take whatever work he could get to feed his family.

Later, after Addy had helped Momma wash the supper dishes, Poppa said, "Addy, you want to come with me to take the covers off the furniture in Mr. Radisson's house?"

Addy said yes immediately. As she and Poppa walked across the snowy yard toward Mr. Radisson's back porch, she remembered the light and a shiver went through her.

She stood back and watched as Poppa opened the shuttered porch door and went inside. He didn't seem to notice anything worrisome. With a glance over each shoulder, Addy joined him on the porch.

Poppa knelt down by a small table and said, "Come over here, Addy. I want to show you something."

Addy knelt down beside Poppa.

"Look at this workmanship," he said. "I'd like to make some fancy tables just like this someday."

Addy ran her hands along the curved mahogany table with lions carved on it. A stab of pain shot through her finger. She said, "Ouch."

Poppa grabbed her hand. "You all right?"

Addy said, "I got a splinter."

"Let's go inside where there's more light and I'll get it out," Poppa said. The door that led to the house was locked. Poppa took a key from the lintel over the door and opened it.

As Poppa waved Addy inside, he stopped and looked at the window to the right of the door. "I thought I shut that window just this morning," he said. "Don't let me forget it on the way out."

In the kitchen, Poppa turned on a gas lamp and

held Addy's finger near the light. "I think I see that splinter. It's a pretty nasty one, too," he said, pulling the sliver of wood from Addy's finger. "Get your momma to put some salve on it when we get back home."

Addy smiled. It was nice to hear Poppa describe the pretty house as home.

Poppa smiled back. "Ready to get to work?"

Addy walked close behind Poppa as he went farther into the huge kitchen. But the beauty of the room soon made her forget her uneasiness. Most kitchens Addy had seen were dark and dreary, but this one had three windows that opened onto the porch. She whistled.

Poppa said, "Sam sure taught you to whistle good, Addy."

The room was cold. Addy shivered. "What's that, Poppa?" she asked, pointing to a large cabinet. "That thing with a pan under it?"

"Want me to riddle you?"

Addy grinned. "Yes, yes, yes," Addy said. "You know I love riddles, Poppa."

"What's solid and liquid?" Poppa asked. "And you can chew it and drink it?"

Addy twisted her mouth from side to side, thinking. *Hmm.* "I know, I know—ice," she shouted with triumph.

Poppa laughed. "That's right. And this is an icebox. Your brother has really taught you to riddle good. You gonna make a fine teacher someday. Now come on this way. We gonna do the front parlor and the dining room tonight."

Addy gave the kitchen a last glance before turning to follow Poppa. For a second, she thought she saw a shadow cross the open window. At that moment, Addy realized that this was where she'd seen the light last night—here in the kitchen. "Wait for me," Addy called. She walked so close behind Poppa that she stepped on the heel of his boot.

As Addy and Poppa walked through the silent

house, she could see that it was grander than Master Stevens's house. Gas lamps hung from the walls in every room. The walls had designs of pretty gold flowers that looked as if they'd been painted on. The flowered carpet stretched from one end of the floor to the other.

Poppa worked alongside Addy, lifting the white covers from the furniture and folding them.

"Poppa," Addy asked as she folded the last cover. "Do you believe in ghosts?"

Poppa straightened a chair. "I reckon so, Addy."

Addy felt a tightening in her chest. She hadn't thought Poppa's answer would be that. "You think they real?" Addy said.

"I seen a ghost once, long time 'go. When I was a boy," Poppa said. "I heard it, too."

"Poppa, can we go now?" Addy asked.

The minute Poppa nodded, Addy was out the back door.

"Are you all right?" Poppa called after her.

Addy said yes, but she didn't feel all right. If Poppa had seen a ghost, then maybe she had, too.

Addy couldn't sleep that night. She listened to Esther's soft breathing and wished she could go to sleep as quickly as her little sister. Thoughts of the ghost rumbled around in her mind. Mr. Radisson's uncle had died in that house. Was his restless spirit haunting it now?

chapter 5
A Cold Welcome

AS SHE WALKED up the street on her way home from school the next day, Addy studied Mr. Radisson's house. It stood tall and silent in the late-afternoon shadows. All the windows were dark. Addy shivered. She wished Mr. Radisson would get back from Virginia.

Just then, a fancy black carriage pulled up in front of the house. Addy spotted the top of Mr. Radisson's hat as he climbed out of the carriage.

"Addy," he called. "Come over. I have someone I'd like you to meet." He went around to the other side of the carriage.

Addy hurried to join him, but then stopped in surprise. She couldn't tell whether it was a bird or a bear standing beside Mr. Radisson. It was short, had a big chest, and was furry. A bird perched on top, with long, fancy feathers sticking out.

"Addy, this is my mother, Mrs. Radisson. Mother, this is Addy Walker. Her family just moved into the servants' house."

"How do you do, ma'am?" Addy said.

"I'm freezing," replied Mrs. Radisson brusquely, her features seeming to pinch close together. She turned to her son. "Albert, I need to get out of the cold."

Mr. Radisson took his mother's elbow, giving Addy an apologetic smile. As they headed toward the house, Mrs. Radisson's scolding voice carried through the chilly air. "I told you specifically to hire an English couple. If you were going to settle for coloreds, you could have kept the ones your uncle had."

In a low voice, Mr. Radisson said sharply, "Mother, that is the young girl who saved my life. And her family are not servants. Addy's father works for me as a skilled carpenter."

"Nonsense. What do you mean, they aren't servants? They're colored, aren't they? Land sakes, your northern winters are cold. I can't wait until this wedding is over so that I can return to Virginia."

Watching them disappear into the house, Addy thought, *I didn't know bears got cold.*

That evening, just after supper, Addy's family gathered in the sitting room. Poppa snored lightly in a chair. Sam read a book. Esther played with Janie. Momma sewed pearls onto a dress, her last piece of work from Mrs. Ford. Addy had just started studying her Latin book when a knock sounded on the door.

Poppa went to the door and came back with Mr. Radisson.

"Good evening, folks," Mr. Radisson said.

Poppa introduced him to the family. "This is my wife, Ruth Walker, and my son, Sam. This is my little Esther," Poppa said, lifting Esther into his arms. "And you remember Addy."

Sam, Esther, and Addy said, "Good evening, sir."

Momma shook Mr. Radisson's hand.

Mr. Radisson said, "Nice to meet you. You certainly have a strong little girl here, Mrs. Walker. She knocked me down hard," he added, chuckling.

Momma smiled and said, "Thank you, sir. Oh, I don't mean thank you that Addy knocked you down."

Mr. Radisson laughed. So did Momma and Poppa.

Then Mr. Radisson noticed the dress Momma had been working on. "That's a lovely gown," he said. "Did you make that, Mrs. Walker?"

"Yes, Momma made it," Addy said. "She can sew real good."

"Really well," Sam said, correcting Addy.

Addy said quickly, "Really well. I mean, Momma can sew really well. She worked at Mrs. Ford's dress shop for two years."

"That shop had an excellent reputation!" Mr. Radisson clapped his hands. "Then it's settled—that is, if you agree. My fiancée arrives from Connecticut in a few days for our wedding next month, and I'd love to tell her I've found the perfect person to alter the wedding dress. You see, she agreed sight unseen to wear my mother's gown, but it will need to be altered to fit her, and she's requested lace, ribbons, and jewels on it in the latest style. Unfortunately, my mother's dress has none of the above. Would you be willing to take the job, Mrs. Walker?"

"I don't mind, sir," Momma said, "but I never altered a wedding dress before. I just don't know if I can do it."

Addy squeezed Momma's hand. "You can, Momma. I know you can."

"Your employment with Mrs. Ford speaks highly for your abilities, Mrs. Walker," said Mr. Radisson with a reassuring smile. "When I return from my trip, I'll drop off the dress and some decorative materials I picked out in Paris at my fiancée's request."

Addy didn't mean to speak out loud, but she heard herself say, "You've been to Paris, sir?"

"Yes, many times. You would love it there, Addy," Mr. Radisson said. "Maybe you'll get to visit Paris yourself one day."

Addy couldn't even imagine going to Paris. She stood staring at Mr. Radisson. Then she reminded herself: She couldn't have imagined this house only a few weeks before. Maybe she *would* one day go to Paris. Now that she and her family were free, nothing was impossible.

When she turned her attention back to the conversation, Mr. Radisson was saying to Momma, "This works out perfectly. My fiancée will be eager to meet you. Would you come to my house on Saturday for tea? Bring Addy with you."

Addy's mouth dropped open, and so did Momma's. They were being invited to tea at a white man's house? "Why, thank you, sir," Momma said.

Then Mr. Radisson turned to Poppa, and his face became serious. "Mr. Walker, I heard about what's been going on at work. I'm so sorry. I'm leaving for Connecticut tomorrow, but I'll see if I can't settle the problem with Mr. Gunter when I return."

That night Esther slept soundly, but Addy couldn't quiet her own thoughts. Restless, she knelt by the window and looked out at Mr. Radisson's house. A gaslight lit one of the upstairs windows, but after a few minutes it went dark. Addy waited for a while, but nothing else happened. The only thing outside was the darkness and snow.

The next night, Addy kept watch at the window again. Once again the house stayed dark. Addy began to relax. Now that the house was occupied, maybe the ghost had left. Or maybe she had only imagined the light, or even dreamed it . . .

After a while, Addy could barely keep her eyes open, her left leg went numb, and her body felt heavy as lead. Addy crawled under the covers and slept more soundly than she had all week.

Sometime later in the night, piercing screams jolted her awake.

Addy leaped to the window. Mrs. Radisson stood at the porch door in a black robe and a puffy black silk bonnet, holding up a lantern and scream-ing, "Help! Thief!"

Addy heard Poppa and Sam racing out of the house. She jumped up and ran after them. They both were in their long johns and bare feet. Poppa yelled to Mrs. Radisson, "What's happening?"

Mrs. Radisson pointed toward the wrought-iron gate, swinging back and forth at the entrance to the alley. "He went that way. Catch him!"

Poppa and Sam ran toward the gate.

Momma came out onto the porch, holding Poppa's and Sam's boots. Mrs. Radisson was still shouting.

After a few minutes, Addy and Momma watched Poppa and Sam trudging back to the porch. Addy and Momma hurried to Poppa and Sam to give them their boots.

Poppa said, "Sorry, ma'am, but we didn't see anyone." He bent over to put on his boots.

"Of course you didn't," Mrs. Radisson huffed. "I've no doubt it was a colored man. Well, when Albert gets back, I will see that the police are notified."

Sam asked, "What exactly happened, ma'am?" Addy held Sam's arm for balance as he struggled with his boots.

"I was in the kitchen getting some milk when I heard a noise out here on the porch," Mrs. Radisson said. "I gathered up my lamp and came out. There was no one on the porch, but I looked out and saw the back gate swinging back and forth as if someone had just lit out—a thief, I tell you!"

"Ma'am?" Poppa asked. "So you saw the colored man running down the alley?"

"Aren't you listening?" Mrs. Radisson said. "I didn't see anyone. But I found this basket by the door. Someone was trying to get away with some cheese, bread, and preserves," she added, holding up her evidence. In the moonlight, Addy could even see the blue and red design woven into the basket's rim. "The thief must have dropped it when I surprised him."

"Cheese, bread, and preserves?" Momma said. "I don't understand. Why would a thief break into your house and then steal nothing but cheese, bread, and preserves?"

"What right have you to question me?" Mrs. Radisson snapped. She turned and went back into the house, muttering, "It wouldn't surprise me if it was one of you."

After the door slammed shut, Poppa picked up the basket and looked inside. "It has food in it, all right. I don't know who tried to take this, but that woman sure doesn't know whether it was a colored person or not."

Sam said, "Let's take that food home and examine it—in our stomachs."

Momma shook her head. "No. Leave it be. She'll find some way to blame us if it's missing. I've seen people like this before, thinking everything wrong in the world is caused by colored people. Let's just all get back to bed."

Poppa set the basket down on the step. "I sure don't envy Mr. Radisson," he said.

Addy spent the rest of the night tossing in bed. What if it was a ghost that Mrs. Radisson had heard? Did ghosts eat food? Addy didn't know, but she did want to take a look at that basket.

At first light, Addy checked out the window. There was no sign of Mrs. Radisson. The big house looked dark and quiet.

Addy slipped downstairs and drew on her shawl. She carefully opened the door and stepped out into the cold. She looked across the shadowy yard one more time for any sign of Mrs. Radisson. Then Addy bent low, running for the porch. She hoped no one would see her.

She was surprised to find that the basket was gone.

After school, as Addy walked up to the back gate, she spotted the red-and-blue–trimmed basket atop a pile of trash in the alley. Addy picked up the basket and looked inside. The food was still there. Addy couldn't believe that Mrs. Radisson had thrown the food away instead of offering it to someone.

Addy glanced toward Mr. Radisson's house. Would Poppa be mad if Addy took the basket? She didn't think so. Poppa and Momma didn't think people should waste food.

Addy hurried into the kitchen. The house was quiet. That meant Momma was lying down taking a nap with Esther. *Good,* Addy thought. She wanted to look at the basket alone.

She set it on the table and bent close to examine it. It looked like an everyday straw basket, round with two handles. Addy removed the food from the basket—a hunk of hard cheese wrapped in a cloth, half a loaf of bread, and a jar of preserves. She turned the empty basket upside down and shook it. She didn't know what she expected, but she felt a twinge of disappointment when only a few bread crumbs fell out. Addy poked the cloth lining of the basket. Nothing there.

Addy was just about to put the food back into the basket when she noticed a tiny bit of paper wedged between the cloth and the straw bottom. Gently Addy tried to pry the paper out. The paper didn't move—but the bottom of the basket did. Addy pushed at it with her finger, and suddenly the entire bottom of the basket came out, a tightly woven straw disk. Below it was the real bottom of the basket. Pressed against the coiled straw was a tiny, crumpled slip of paper.

Addy stared. The basket had a fake bottom. She had never seen a basket like this.

Carefully, Addy removed the crumpled paper and spread it out. On the torn and yellowed paper, someone had drawn several rows of angles and dots in heavy black ink. The markings made no sense at all to Addy. Her heart thudded.

What was this paper? And why on earth would a basket have a fake bottom? There was only one reason—to hide something.

Suddenly Addy heard Momma calling from upstairs, "Addy? Addy, you home?"

"Yes, Momma," Addy said, putting the false bottom back into place. Quickly she stuck the scrap of paper into her pocket.

A moment later, Momma walked into the kitchen. "Why do you have that basket?"

Addy told Momma where she'd gotten it. She didn't mention the false bottom. "Can I keep it?" she asked.

Momma nodded but said, "For now, put it in the shed."

That night, when the house was quiet, Addy got up and perched at her bedroom window. She didn't know what the angles and dots on that hidden slip of paper could mean, but now she felt sure that something strange was going on at Mr. Radisson's house.

Addy watched the house for a long time. She fought to keep her eyes open. She had no idea what time it happened, but finally she saw the light appear—not in the kitchen window this time, but on the porch.

Addy saw the light grow brighter and higher. Then it moved across the porch, flickering through the shutter slats. Addy peered up at Mrs. Radisson's window, but it was dark. Every window in the house was pitch-black.

The porch door opened slowly. Addy caught her breath. She fingered the protection stone that Uncle Solomon had given Sam. She waited.

A hand emerged from the doorway, down low near the step. The hand, dark against the snow, seemed to move around on the step. Then, just as quickly, the hand was gone.

The door closed. The light grew dimmer and, just as before, suddenly sank down and disappeared.

Addy shivered. Had she really seen a hand—
a ghost's hand? When Addy finally went to sleep,
she dreamed about angles, dots, and baskets.

On her way to school the next morning, Addy
stopped by the porch, but she didn't see anything
out of place. She began to walk away, but then
turned, went back to the porch, and knelt by
the step.

She could see markings in the snow where
fingers had swept along the snowy surface, as if
searching for something. What? The basket?

Addy bent closer to the step. Ghosts did not
leave prints. Maybe there was no ghost but a real
person hiding in Mr. Radisson's house.

Addy peered through the open wooden slats
onto the porch. What if that person was watching
her right now? Addy took off running.

chapter 6

The Mystery Woman

AUNTIE LULA ALWAYS said, *Everything that's done in the dark comes out into the light.* When Addy came through the back gate after school on Friday, she heard Mrs. Radisson calling, "You, girl, come here."

Addy crossed the yard to the porch. Mrs. Radisson stood in the kitchen doorway. "Did you steal my milk?" she asked.

"No, ma'am," Addy said.

"Don't fib. Did you take the milk? I set it here on the step last night because it was colder outside than in the icebox. When I came out to get the milk this morning, it was gone."

"Ma'am, I didn't take it," Addy said.

Mrs. Radisson's eyes narrowed. "You sure

about that?" she asked.

Addy nodded.

"All right. But I'm warning you. Ever since I got here, things have been going missing." Mrs. Radisson went back inside and shut the door with a bang.

Addy stared at the door. Mrs. Radisson wasn't the only one who would be happy when the wedding was over and she went home. Addy wondered if the mystery person had taken the milk. She was about to step off the porch when she thought she saw movement near the table. She whirled around. Nothing.

Addy scanned the interior of the porch. Everything looked exactly as it had when she and Poppa had come over to remove the cloths from the furniture. Everything was the same ... except for one small detail. Now a tiny piece of bright orange yarn dangled from a corner of the carved mahogany table.

Addy stepped closer to examine it. The yarn had caught on the same nick in the wood where the splinter had jabbed into Addy's finger. But where had the yarn come from? Addy picked it up and rolled it between her fingers. She couldn't imagine Mrs. Radisson wearing anything so brightly colored. Someone was sneaking onto the porch. Addy needed to find out who—before she and her family ended up in trouble.

She made up her mind. After dark, she would come back to the porch to look for clues. After tonight, two more people would be in the house—Mr. Radisson and his fiancée. If Addy was going to do this, tonight was the time.

Addy stayed awake until the neighborhood was dark and still. Then she hugged her shawl around her shoulders, slipped out into the cold, and raced across the yard. If someone came to the porch tonight, she planned to be close enough to see every detail. On the right side of the porch, she found a spot where one of the shutter slats was broken. She cupped her hands and pressed against the opening. It provided a good angle. She could see the kitchen door, the window above the table, and the porch door. Addy waited.

Her fingers had gone numb before she finally dozed off, resting her head on one of the slats. She dreamed she heard a screeching sound followed by a thud, then scraping.

Addy woke in fright to see a woman's silhouette standing before her on the porch. Addy didn't know if the woman had come through the kitchen door or window or the porch door. But there she was, facing right toward Addy. Addy ducked down, knocking snow off the vines on the trellis. The snow cascaded onto her, as if it were once again falling from the sky.

Crouched on the ground, Addy peered through

the shutters and almost gasped aloud. Now she
could see that it was a colored woman—a colored
woman holding something in her hands. Was she
taking something else from the house? Addy could
barely breathe. She faintly heard the woman's footsteps moving on the porch, and then the squeak
of the porch door opening and the sound of a boot
on the step.

Addy was too scared to peek around the corner.
She clutched the protection stone. She was sure the
woman had seen her. What would the woman do
if she caught Addy?

Addy decided in a split second to run. She
sprang forward, racing across the yard toward
home. She had just made it to the front door when
she realized that the woman wasn't behind her—
she was walking briskly toward the shed! Addy
couldn't believe it. Had the woman not seen her
after all?

Addy shivered from the cold and realized that

her shawl was gone. She saw that it had caught on the side of the porch when she ran. Gusts of wind scattered snow across the expanse of the yard.

Addy saw the shed door closing. The woman had gone inside.

Addy wondered if she should wake Poppa. No—first she should see what the woman had taken. Then Addy would fetch Poppa and Mrs. Radisson, and they could catch the thief red-handed.

Addy took a few deep breaths. She couldn't be afraid. She had been in danger before, from much worse than this. And, Addy realized, if the woman had stolen only food, she didn't think she could call Mrs. Radisson. Not for food. Addy knew what it felt like to be hungry. She'd just get Poppa to warn the woman away.

Addy remembered exactly where the windows were in the shed. Quickly, she made her way to the shed and peered inside.

For a moment, she saw only darkness. Then a small flame flared, and Addy saw the woman light a white candle and stick it securely in the dirt floor. The flickering flame made a circle of light in the blackness. Addy was glad. Whatever the woman had taken, Addy would see it now. She gripped the window ledge harder, waiting.

Addy couldn't believe what she saw next.

The woman seated herself on the floor near the candle and held up two lemon halves, as though she were on a stage giving a performance. Then she removed a small jar from underneath her brown and orange shawl.

The orange in the shawl matched the yarn Addy had found earlier. Now Addy knew the woman had been on the porch before tonight.

Addy watched as the woman squeezed lemon juice into the jar. Then she took a thin, small stick from her pocket.

The woman dipped the stick into the lemon

juice. She began writing something on a piece of paper with the stick. Addy watched as the woman's hand moved across and back several times.

When the woman was done, she threw the lemon halves to the ground and carefully put the stick into a small leather bag. She wiped her hands on a handkerchief and returned it to her pocket. She waved the paper a few times and then—

The light went out.

Addy ran to get Poppa. But halfway across the yard, she began to slow her pace. Nothing she had seen made sense. What would she tell Poppa? That she'd seen a woman appear on the porch from nowhere, go into the shed and squeeze some lemons, and then disappear?

Addy stood still, wrapping her arms around herself against the cold. Then she walked back to the shed, determined to ask the woman to stop taking things and leave. After all, Sam had said that she was very brave.

A lantern hung beside the shed door. Addy took it down and grabbed the matches beside it. "Hello?" she called softly, stepping into the shed. "I saw you. I know you're in here." Addy could feel her heart crashing up against her chest. She squeezed Uncle Solomon's smooth stone in her fingers. "I know you're in here," she repeated.

Addy knelt and lit the lantern. The only thing she saw was the two lemon halves. There was no one in the shed—but one of the windows was slung wide open. Addy stomped the floor. She'd let the woman escape. What now?

Addy suddenly felt not only cold but exhausted. She put out the lantern, hung it back on the hook, and shut the shed door. She looked at Mr. Radisson's house. The morning light would come soon. Addy needed to get home before Poppa and Momma got up, or worse, before Mrs. Radisson caught her snooping. There was no telling what the mystery woman had taken from the house.

Addy spotted her shawl, lying rumpled in the snow. She thought the wind must have blown it. If Poppa or Momma saw it, she would have a hard time explaining why it was out there. Addy ran to get it. She grabbed the shawl and turned toward her house. The sound of something falling and hitting the ground made her stop and look back.

Lying on the ground were the small leather bag and the candle. Addy couldn't even blink. *Why?* Why had the woman put these things inside Addy's shawl? Did she want Mrs. Radisson to blame Addy for taking them? Where was the woman now? Addy looked at the house, the shed, and the gate, but there was no sign of her.

Addy picked up the bag and opened it. Just as she feared, everything was there: the stick, the jar, the paper—and, to her surprise, a whole lemon. Addy thought to just leave it all. But she wanted to see what the woman had written on the paper. Maybe it was a confession. Addy quickly looked around to make sure no one saw her, wrapped everything in her shawl, and hurried home.

Addy slipped into her room, careful not to disturb her sister, and sat on her bed. The sun's light was peeping over the horizon, warming the earth outside. Addy couldn't stop her fingers from shaking as she opened the bag and pulled the paper out. She laid the bag to the side. The paper was intricately folded, one fold on top of another, almost like a paper trick she'd seen once where the folded paper was cut up and then pulled open to reveal the shape of an animal.

Addy took a deep breath. What had the woman written? Who was the message for?

Carefully Addy unfolded the paper. She had never seen paper like this—so thin she could see through it, and puffy in spots. She decided that after she read it, she would take it to Poppa. As she opened the paper, she could feel sweat on her top lip, even though she still shivered from being outside in the cold.

Addy held the paper up to the light coming through the window. Her eyes widened and her hand flew to her mouth. She felt as if she would vomit.

Addy had clearly seen the woman writing on the paper with the stick dipped in lemon juice, back and forth for at least a few lines. But now there was no message on the paper. There was only one word, scrawled not in pale lemon juice but in bold black ink—and it was the last word Addy ever expected to see there. She had never thought she could be scared of one word. But she was.

Addy lay down on her bed. She wondered if Uncle Solomon's stone could really protect her. She curled into a ball, still clutching the thin sheet of paper, while the one word written on it pounded in her brain:

ADDY

chapter 7
The Black Swan

ADDY DID HER Saturday chores without thinking about them. While she dusted furniture and polished the gas lamps and swept the floors, her mind saw nothing but that paper with her name scrawled on it. Whenever she caught herself looking out at Mr. Radisson's house, she forced her eyes away. She didn't want Momma asking questions.

She even forgot about having tea at Mr. Radisson's until Momma said, "Addy, it's 'bout time you got ready. Wash up now and put on your Sunday clothes." Momma curtseyed like a fancy lady.

Ordinarily Momma's gesture would have made Addy laugh. But right now, the last place

Addy wanted to be was in Mr. Radisson's house. "I'm feeling tired, Momma," Addy said. "Do I have to go?"

"Yes, you have to go." Momma put her hand on Addy's shoulder. "Don't be nervous. Mr. Radisson is a nice man. Now get ready."

Addy nodded to Momma, then hurried to her room and washed up. But the entire time, all she could think about was her name written bold and black on the paper.

As soon as Addy and Momma had dressed, Momma sat down in the parlor to sew while they waited for Mr. Radisson's knock. She made Addy sit quietly on the settee.

The rest of the family gathered in the parlor with them. Poppa and Sam were going to watch Esther while Momma and Addy went to tea. Esther was busy begging Momma to let her come along, while Momma ripped the seams from one of Addy's old dresses so that Esther could wear it.

Addy still couldn't believe Mr. Radisson had invited them to tea. A colored family invited to a white family's tea! Even Mrs. Ford had never invited Addy and Momma to eat with her the whole time she'd known them.

Until last night, Addy had been excited to meet the woman who would marry Mr. Radisson. Now she was just plain anxious. Addy fidgeted in her seat, sighing heavily each time Momma looked up from her sewing.

Despite her nerves, Addy realized that she was still curious about Mr. Radisson's fiancée. Addy clutched the protection stone and hoped it truly worked. Her stomach flipped when the knock came at the door.

Poppa answered the door and let Mr. Radisson into the kitchen. Addy could hear the two of them exchanging pleasantries. Finally Mr. Radisson stepped into the parlor. "Good afternoon," he said. "Are you ladies ready for tea?"

"Yes, sir," Addy replied politely. Momma had told her she was to be on her best behavior. Momma didn't want white people thinking that colored people didn't know how to act.

Addy and Momma put on their shawls and walked alongside Mr. Radisson across the yard. Addy stayed close to Momma as they crossed the porch and went into the house.

With the afternoon light spilling through the windows, Mr. Radisson's house looked more beautiful than any house Addy had ever seen. Mr. Radisson directed Addy and Momma to the dining room. "My mother is taking another engagement this afternoon and won't be here," he said, pulling out two chairs for them. "Make yourselves at home. I shall return shortly."

Addy and Momma settled down at the dining table with their hands in their laps. Addy noticed that the table was covered with a beautiful tablecloth of thick white lace. In the middle of the table, a crystal vase held a bouquet of blue and yellow flowers, and on each side of it were fine china plates painted with bluebirds. The plates held wafers, muffins, and tea cakes set atop white linen doilies.

Momma smiled encouragingly at Addy. Addy attempted to push thoughts of the mystery woman out of her mind. But every few minutes, her own name would flash in front of her eyes just the way it had been written on the paper.

Mr. Radisson and his fiancée entered the room. Addy felt immediately charmed by the young woman's beauty. She was tiny for a grown woman, almost the same size as Addy. Her long hair was dark, like her eyes. She wore an elegant dress of peach lace with black velvet trim.

Mr. Radisson introduced Miss Elizabeth Waring Cope to Momma and Addy.

"It's a pleasure to meet you both," she said, smiling warmly.

Addy thought, *She has the most beautiful voice.*
It sounded like the chimes at church. Addy admired
Miss Elizabeth's long black lashes. She was the most
beautiful white woman Addy had ever seen.

Addy found it fun to lift the delicate teacups
into the air—they reminded her of butterflies for
some reason. She watched Miss Elizabeth's every
move and tried her best to hold her cup exactly the
same way. Addy smiled when she saw Momma was
holding her pinky out, too.

Addy took a bite of a tea cake. It was very good.
She was about to take another bite when she realized Miss Elizabeth was talking to her.

"Addy, Albert tells me that you are a brave girl
and that you saved his life. I want you to know that
I am so grateful."

Addy felt the blood rushing to her face. "You're
welcome," she said.

"He also told me that you wouldn't take any
reward. How admirable."

Addy said, "Thank you." Then she thought she saw Mr. Radisson wink at Miss Elizabeth.

"How would you like to attend a marvelous concert, Addy?" Mr. Radisson asked. "I just happen to have two tickets." He reached into his pocket and pulled out the tickets. "Addy, you and your mother could go. It's an opportunity for ladies to put on their finest dresses. The Black Swan herself will be performing."

Addy sat up straight.

"Who is the Black Swan?" Momma asked.

"Allow me, please," Miss Elizabeth said. "Her real name is Elizabeth Greenfield."

"Just like yours," Addy said.

Miss Elizabeth smiled. "Yes. The Black Swan is one of the first colored women to perform opera. She was schooled in Europe by Queen Victoria's own organist and did a command performance for the queen."

"The miraculous part of the story," Mr. Radisson

added, "is that she was once a slave."

Addy looked at Mr. Radisson in amazement.

"It's true, Addy," Miss Elizabeth said. "Years ago, her Quaker owner gave her freedom when they moved to Philadelphia. Her former owner even paid for her to take music lessons."

Momma shook her head in disbelief.

From behind them, Addy heard a soft rustling. Instantly, her mind flashed on the image of the paper with her name on it. She couldn't believe she'd forgotten about it. Was the mystery woman here right now, watching her?

Addy turned toward the sound and saw Mrs. Radisson walking into the room. Her dark gray silk gown rustled with each step.

"What have we here, Albert? I wondered what you were up to." Her gray hair was tied up in a bun. "Trying to shuffle me off?"

Mr. Radisson rose. "Please join us, Mother."

"No, thank you. I have better things to do with

my time. Elizabeth, I hope you will talk some sense into my son. He's getting to be just like his Abolitionist uncle."

Addy saw Miss Elizabeth lower her head, her beautiful face as red as if she'd been turned upside down.

Mr. Radisson held out his hand to his mother. "Would you like me to see you to your room?"

"No, thank you," Mrs. Radisson said sharply. "I think you've done rather enough."

When his mother had gone, Mr. Radisson said, "I find that I am constantly apologizing for my mother. Let's get on to more pleasant conversation. She'll be fine." Mr. Radisson took Miss Elizabeth's delicate hand in his. "My dear," he said, "I have a surprise for you."

Miss Elizabeth pressed her lips together as if to compose herself. "Yes?" she said.

"Mrs. Walker here is a fine seamstress. She has agreed to make the alterations on the wedding gown," Mr. Radisson continued. "I think you will love her handiwork."

"Oh, Albert, that is a nice surprise!" Miss Elizabeth said delightedly. "I almost thought you'd forgotten about the dress." She smiled at Momma. "You know how men can be about things of this nature. Mrs. Walker, may I come over on Monday for a fitting?"

"Yes, of course," Momma answered. "That will be fine."

"Speaking of dresses," Miss Elizabeth said, "one of my favorite dresses doesn't fit me anymore. I was planning to give it to charity, but I would be much happier if I could see Addy wearing it. With the hem taken up and perhaps a few silk flowers added for embellishment, it would be perfect for someone Addy's age."

Addy squeezed her eyes shut. She thought, *Momma, please say yes. Please.*

Mr. Radisson said, "That sounds like the perfect

dress for Addy to wear to the concert. What do you say, Mrs. Walker?"

"That's so generous of you both," Momma said. "But—but I couldn't accept it."

Addy looked at Momma, pleading with her eyes.

Momma hesitated. "Well, I suppose . . . Addy certainly deserves a new dress. All right, yes. And thank you."

"Then it's settled," Mr. Radisson said, grinning.

Soon the tea came to an end. Addy left the room in a glow of excitement.

But when she stepped through the kitchen door onto the porch, just like a cloud that covers the moon, fear washed over Addy. All of a sudden, the only thing flashing in Addy's mind was her name on the piece of paper.

chapter 8
A Strange Riddle

THAT NIGHT ADDY could not sleep.
Every time she closed her eyes, she saw her name
scrawled on the sheet of paper. Inside her stomach,
it felt like butter was being churned.

Before dawn, Addy got up and took her doll,
Ida Bean, from the trunk at the foot of her bed.
Momma had given Ida Bean to Addy on their first
Christmas in Philadelphia. Addy hugged Ida close,
just as she used to. She whispered to Ida Bean,
"I'm sorry I put you in the trunk. From now on, you
sleep with me."

Finally Addy closed her eyes and slept. But
Sunday morning came all too soon.

As the Walkers set out for church, they saw Mr.
Radisson, Mrs. Radisson, and Miss Elizabeth getting

into a carriage. "Have a good day," Mr. Radisson called to Poppa. "We'll be back late tonight."

All through church and Sunday dinner, Addy could not keep her mind off the mystery woman's paper. She was relieved when Poppa suggested they all go for a walk after dinner.

"Poppa," she said, "I'm tired. Can I stay home?" She *was* tired, but mostly she wanted time alone to look for clues in the things the woman had left in Addy's shawl.

Momma said, "Let her stay, Ben. She's been looking a little peaked lately."

Poppa hesitated. "Addy would be alone."

Addy quickly said, "Poppa, I'll be fine."

"She's right," Momma said. "Addy is growing up. Let her stay."

The minute they left, Addy raced upstairs. From under her bed, she pulled out the candle and the leather bag. She removed the bag's contents and laid everything out on the floor—the lemon, the stick, the jar, and the paper.

Suddenly she had an idea. She ran to the kitchen and came back with a knife and cut the lemon in half. She took a sheet of paper from her book sack and tried to repeat exactly what she'd seen the woman do. But nothing happened. Now she just had wet paper.

Addy needed another idea. She picked up the candle. It looked like an ordinary candle. Why had the woman left it for her? Addy got a match and lit the candle. It burned the way all candles do, the flickering flame casting shadows on the walls. *The candle must be important,* Addy thought. *But why?*

Frustrated, she picked up the paper that the woman had written on. She looked at both sides, turning the paper this way and that.

She held the paper close to the candle flame so that she could see it better. Suddenly a mark appeared on the paper that hadn't been there before. She held the thin paper even closer to the flame. More marks appeared. Addy moved the paper over

the candle's flame, back and forth, holding it as
close as she could without burning it. Sure enough,
words formed on the paper, one line at a time.
Addy's hands trembled as she read.

Dear Addy,

*You are a smart girl. I need your help. Like a
runaway slave I need your help. I'm in danger.*

*Find me where the sun meets the sky, but by
going under the wooden door, not in the wall but
in the floor.*

Addy remembered how scared she had been
when she and Momma ran for freedom. Addy
could almost feel the heat of fear swelling inside as
they were making their way through the woods...
Momma almost drowning... Addy shaking inside
when she pretended to be a boy in the Confederate
soldiers' camp. Addy knew what danger was,
and she didn't want anyone else to feel such fear.

Maybe—maybe she would help the woman.

Addy took a deep breath and curled her fingers around the protection stone.

She read the note again. Like all riddles, this one didn't make sense. *Where the sun meets the sky.* Addy moved past those words. She had learned to always start at the end of a riddle. *The floor.* Addy thought, *That's it.* Whatever she should look for, it was in the floor. *A door.* Look for a door in the floor.

Then what? How would the sun meet the sky?

Addy thought hard. She considered everything that had happened so far—the basket of food being stolen, the slip of paper with the strange dots and angles, the milk missing from the step. She thought back to the first time she had been in the kitchen with Poppa, and how she thought she'd seen a shadow. And she remembered that Poppa had thought he'd closed the kitchen window that opened onto the porch. She remembered that the orange piece of yarn caught on the table matched the shawl that the woman had worn two nights ago. Most of the incidents had happened on the porch. Now she knew where to look first.

Just then, Addy heard her family coming home. She hurried to put everything away.

Addy had barely shoved the bag under her bed before Momma walked into the room, carrying Esther. "You awake, Addy?" she said. "The rest of us are tuckered out. We're all gonna take naps."

The minute Momma said that, Addy saw her opportunity. As her family settled down to rest, Addy ran across the yard to Mr. Radisson's house. She opened the door and stepped onto the porch as quietly as possible. Even though she knew no one was home, she paused a second to listen. Then she got to work.

Where would the sun meet the sky? Addy turned in a slow circle, surveying the porch. Her eyes followed the bars of sunlight shining through the slats of the shutters. The light landed on the table. Addy's heart raced. A lantern and a box of matches sat on the table. Addy was positive of two things: The lantern and the matches had not been there before; and the lantern was the same one that she had used in the shed.

Addy moved closer to the table, which sat on a round rug. She lifted the rug. There in the floorboards, Addy spotted a difference in the wood. *This has to be it—the door in the floor,* she thought. But how did it meet the sky?

Addy smiled. The faded scene on the rug showed a blue sky. The sunlight filtering through the broken slat hit exactly on the sky.

Addy carefully moved the table. She glanced around to make sure that no one was in the yard. She peeped inside the kitchen door to make sure the house was quiet.

Addy folded back the rug. She pulled up the

door in the floor—and looked into the belly of blackness. Fear gripped her stomach. She wiped her forehead. It was pitch-black down below. She would have to use the lantern. Addy went back to the table and picked up the lantern and the matches. Her hands shook. She lit the lantern.

As she stepped slowly down into the darkness, Addy smelled the freshness of wood. Poppa often described it as the pores of the trees bleeding once they were cut. Someone had built these steps not long ago. Addy was sure they weren't as old as the house.

Addy felt her way down the stairs, running her hand along the rough dirt walls on either side as she moved farther into the deep. The light from the lantern didn't show much, just the steps in front of her as she moved down. They seemed to go on for-ever. With every breath, Addy felt Uncle Solomon's protection stone lying on her chest. Once again, she hoped that it really could protect her from danger.

She began to worry that no one would find her if something went wrong. Then she remembered that she'd left the table out of place and the door in the floor open. A second later, her stomach clenched. What if Mr. Radisson came home before she put it all back?

At the foot of the stairs, she saw that she was in some kind of tunnel. Addy couldn't see anything except a long passageway disappearing into darkness. She lifted the light higher. She could barely stand up without the top of the dirt tunnel brushing her hair.

Something scurried across her foot. *What was that?* Addy shuddered and tightened her grip around the lantern's handle, just in case she was startled again. She didn't want to drop the lantern and end up in the dark.

Addy's stomach felt as if someone had lit a fire in it. She found it difficult to breathe as she felt her way along the damp sides of the tunnel. Soon she stumbled into a wall. She stepped back, confused. *Why build a tunnel to no-place?*

There was barely room for Addy to turn around. She held up the lantern and turned slowly. To her right, she saw makeshift stairs, but they went up only six or seven steps. Addy climbed the steps and saw a rope dangling from a board. Cautiously, she pulled the rope. To her surprise, another set of steps appeared above her to her right. She tried to imagine how this passageway fit into the house.

Addy began to climb again. She felt as if the dirt walls were closing in on her. The stairs seemed to go up and up. Addy tried not to make noise as she climbed. All at once, she saw a blinding light. She shielded her eyes and almost fell backward. But she held on to the lantern.

Then she saw it—what looked like a ghostly outstretched hand reaching down to her...
Suddenly everything went blank.

...

She didn't tumble far. Strong hands caught the lantern and Addy's wrist. They pulled her through an opening at the top of the stairs. The faint smell of ammonia caused Addy's eyes to blink. She opened them—and stared into other eyes. Standing over her, holding the lantern, was the mystery woman.

She was brown like Addy. Her hair was long and thick, pulled back from her face. Her eyes were large, and dark brown like her hair. As Addy looked into her face, she could see that the woman was pretty.

"You gave me a scare. You fainted," the woman said. "Here, take a sip of this, Addy."

Addy did not reach for the glass. She curled up, flinching. "How ... how ... do you know my name?"

The woman smiled. "You should be able to guess that. You're a smart girl."

Addy sat up. "You heard my name being called?"

The woman nodded.

Addy said, "I thought you were a ghost."

"I am, in a way."

Addy gasped and hugged her knees. "You're a ghost?"

"Right now, I don't exist. Can you keep a secret?"

"What kind of secret?" Addy asked.

"That's a very thoughtful response. This is an important secret."

"I can't tell my momma and poppa?"

"Addy, you can tell them, just not right now. I need to stay hidden for a few more weeks. Then you can tell them. I need your help."

"Are you a criminal?" Addy asked, hoping she wasn't.

"Some people think so. I was a Union spy."

"But... but... you're a colored woman," Addy said.

"Yes, I am," the woman replied, smiling. "I spied on very important people in the Confederacy. Some even think I embarrassed the Confederate president. So they have a bounty on my head. You would be surprised, Addy, at the number of

Confederates still fighting this war. I need to stay hidden for a while."

Addy struggled to make sense of what she was hearing. "Why are you hiding here?"

"Because of the man who owned this house—Frank Radisson. You see, he was an architect like his nephew, and he was also an Abolitionist. He built this hiding place for escaping slaves. Later, it was used by Union spies." The woman glanced around the small room, furnished with a simple bed and a table and chair, and at the hidden staircase. "When I found myself in danger a few months ago, Frank provided this hiding place. I promised him that I'd stay here until things cooled off. He was in the process of finding a way for me to go to Canada. But then he died suddenly, and now I can't get out to get food."

"But his nephew is a nice man," Addy said. "Why doesn't Mr. Radisson help you?"

"He doesn't know I'm here," the woman

replied. "Addy, I believe he *is* a good man, but
I can't risk his mother finding out about me. If she
knew I was here, she'd turn me in."

Addy agreed. "Then why don't you hide someplace else?" she asked. "Someplace where there are
more colored people?"

"Right now, I have nowhere else to go. And
until last week, this house was the ideal hiding
place. See that uniform?" The woman pointed to
a maid's uniform hanging on a hook in the corner.
"When I needed to go out, I put it on. No one questions a servant in Society Hill. After Frank's death,
his nephew was here only a few nights on and off,
but now that his mother is staying here, I can't go
out." The woman sighed. "A friend that I used to
work with during the war sometimes left food and
messages for me on the porch when he came to
Philadelphia. But as you saw the other night, even
that isn't safe anymore."

Addy still didn't know whether to trust this

strange woman or not. She had never heard of a colored spy. "Why me? Why did you riddle me?"

"Before you arrived here, I overheard Mr. Radisson telling one of his friends that you are a very brave girl because you saved his life. And since you live right here, you can see when it's safe to help me. So I took the chance. Besides," the mystery woman said, looking directly into Addy's eyes and smiling, "I don't have many choices now, do I?"

Addy could hardly believe what she was hearing. From her pocket, she pulled the note that the spy had written her. "How did you make the words on this paper disappear?" Addy asked. "Was it magic?"

"Science. You write with vinegar or lemon juice on onionskin paper. The writing is invisible but, with intense heat, the juice darkens and your message is revealed. You saw how it works, Addy." The spy paused a moment. "Why don't you leave the note here with me now? It will be safer for both of us that way."

Reluctantly, Addy handed her the note. "Where exactly are we?" she asked.

"We're in a hidden room built into the attic. Frank built all kinds of hidden spaces into this house. He was always doing things with architecture that others wouldn't chance. He was a daring man."

"Tell me about your spying," Addy said.

"Later," the mystery woman replied. "You'd better get back."

"One more question. How did you learn to make the writing appear and disappear?"

The woman smiled again. "I'm a spy, Addy. That's what I do. Now, here is some money. If you decide to get me food, please leave it in the back of the shed, behind the stack of wagon parts. You'll know where."

Addy smiled for the first time. The woman

said, "Follow me. I'll show you how to go into the tunnel without being detected."

When they had made their way back to the porch, the spy explained, "There's a rope attached to the rug and another for the hatch door. Once you're on the stairs, you must pull the white rope first to close the hatch door behind you. Then pull the straw rope to move the rug into place."

Addy climbed onto the porch, surprised to find that the sun was still high in the sky. It seemed as if she had been gone for hours.

Addy carried the lantern back to the shed, walking slowly. She needed time to think before she went home. Nothing would be the same anymore. She had met a real-life colored spy—somebody who had helped save the nation. Addy took a deep breath and made her decision. She would help the spy.

As she hung the lantern on its hook, Addy suddenly realized, *She never even told me her name.*

chapter 9

Confusion

ON HER WAY home from school, Addy
stopped at a small corner store and bought cheese
and bread, which she put inside her school sack.
As soon as she walked through the back gate,
Addy slipped into the shed. She found the red-and-
blue–trimmed basket tucked beneath the wagon
parts. She dropped the cheese and bread inside the
basket and put the cloth cover back on top.

When Addy walked into her house, she heard
Miss Elizabeth's laughter even before she saw her.
The laughter was so musical, it made Addy want
to laugh too. She poked her head into the parlor
to say hello.

Miss Elizabeth was standing very straight on
the round stand that Poppa had made for Momma's

sewing station. She was wearing the wedding dress, and Momma was kneeling to adjust the hem. Two lanterns were set nearby to help her see. They were placed on a small table with a top that opened up, where Momma kept her sewing supplies.

"Addy," Momma said, a pin stuck expertly between her lips, "Miss Elizabeth was just saying how pretty you are."

Addy sat down, watching Momma slowly pin up Miss Elizabeth's dress. She couldn't imagine that Mrs. Radisson had ever worn the lovely dress.

"Did you have a good day at school?" Momma asked.

"Yes, Momma," Addy said.

Miss Elizabeth smiled. "Addy, why don't you come over in a few days to try on the dress I have for you. I think you'll like it."

Addy agreed, and Miss Elizabeth added, "I brought you all a little treat today—some delicious tea cakes. They're in the kitchen."

Momma said, "You can have one, Addy, soon as you get Esther up from her nap."

Addy walked upstairs, thinking about Miss Elizabeth and comparing her warmth to the spy's standoffishness.

The next day, Addy could barely focus on her schoolwork. As soon as school let out, she rushed home, stopping on the way to buy apples. When Addy slipped into the shed, she was relieved to see the bread and cheese gone. She put the apples inside the basket and hurried home. But she couldn't stop thinking about the spy.

As soon as everyone was tucked into bed and all the lights were out at Mr. Radisson's, Addy slipped outside and crept onto the porch. She carefully moved the table and disappeared into the passageway under the floor.

The spy thanked Addy for the food she had left. "You can't stay long, though. It's too dangerous."

"I wanted to know more about spying," Addy said. "What's your name? Where did you come from?"

The spy said, "My name is Mary Tucker. But, Addy, I'm sorry, the less you know about me, the safer it is. All I can tell you is that to be a spy, you have to think fast on your feet. Expect anything to go wrong, and be ready."

Addy felt disappointed. She looked around the small room. *Maybe when you're hiding out,* she thought, *you learn to not talk.* Addy told Miss Tucker about the tickets for the Black Swan's concert and about a paper she was writing for school. Miss Tucker listened carefully to everything she said.

Addy wondered if Miss Tucker was ever lonesome. But before she could ask, Miss Tucker said, "It's time you go now. I don't want you to get into trouble."

Reluctantly, Addy said good-bye. She hadn't learned nearly as much as she wanted to know about spying or Miss Tucker.

Addy had just eased the shed door shut the next afternoon when she heard Miss Elizabeth call across the yard, "How are you, Addy?"

Addy's nerves jumped, but she tried to stay calm. "I'm fine," she said, walking over to join Miss Elizabeth. "And you, ma'am?"

"A little lonely. I had no idea Albert would be so busy now. Would you like to come in and have a cup of tea with me?"

Not sure what to say, Addy just nodded and followed her into the kitchen. Addy felt relieved that Miss Elizabeth hadn't asked what she'd been doing in the shed.

"Have a seat," Miss Elizabeth said.

Addy watched as Mr. Radisson's fiancée

brought the tea urn to the small kitchen table. She set a place for Addy and moved the sugar and creamer tray over so that Addy could reach it.

Addy's hand shook as she dipped out sugar.

"Don't be nervous. Mrs. Radisson has gone out. She's joined some ladies' club. Says she can't stay cooped up in this dreaded house all day," Miss Elizabeth said. "I think it's silly how people don't want to sit and eat with colored people, yet they'll let them cook their food." She offered Addy a small silver tray piled with crackers.

Miss Elizabeth told Addy about her bookkeeping job in Connecticut. She described her trip to Paris and said how much she loved buying pretty things. She even told Addy that she was a little nervous about getting married but that she felt lucky to have found such a nice man.

Addy was fascinated by everything Miss Elizabeth said, but she hardly spoke a word herself. She wasn't accustomed to grown-ups talking to her

as if they were friends. Addy was taking a last sip
of tea when she heard Momma calling for her.

Miss Elizabeth smiled. "Come back tomorrow
and try on the dress. We'll have loads of fun."

When Addy got home, she couldn't stop telling
Momma how nice Miss Elizabeth was. She thought
Miss Elizabeth was the nicest grown-up she'd ever
met. Addy didn't say it, but she couldn't help think-
ing that Miss Elizabeth was a lot friendlier than
Miss Tucker.

After school the next day, Addy hurried to buy
food and set it in the shed so that she could go back
to see Miss Elizabeth again. The two of them had
what Miss Elizabeth called "their tea party" before
they went upstairs to see the dress.

Miss Elizabeth led Addy down a long, carpeted
hallway to her room. The first thing Addy noticed
was that the walls were painted with all kinds of
flowers. She touched a few of them. "They look so
pretty," she commented.

"That's called stenciling," Miss Elizabeth said.

They came to a beautiful room. Flowered fabric that matched the wallpaper hung at the windows and was also draped elegantly behind the head of the bed. The bedstead was made of dark wood, with pineapples carved on each post. A mirrored dresser, chest of drawers, and bureau matched the bed, all gleaming with polish. Gold scroll framed the mirror. A fancy leather trunk sat near the window, with the initials *EWC* engraved on it.

Miss Elizabeth walked over to a white dress and a crinoline laid out on the big bed. "This is the dress I think will look wonderful on you," she said. "It doesn't look too grown-up for a young girl. With a few silk flowers added, it will be perfect for your first concert."

It was the most beautiful dress Addy had ever seen in her life.

"This," Miss Elizabeth said, holding up the skirt of the dress, "is corded silk, and the bodice is made with folds and folds of crepe. I like it for you because it's white, and any color of silk flowers will make it look glorious. Don't you think?"

Miss Elizabeth didn't seem to notice that Addy was speechless. "Try it on. Let's see how much it needs to be altered. Put the crinoline on first, and then the dress over it."

Addy walked over to the dress. Her hands shook as she removed her own clothes. She turned her back so Miss Elizabeth couldn't see her mended undergarments. She put on the crinoline skirt and tied it snugly around her waist. Then she slipped her arms into the dress.

"Lovely," Miss Elizabeth said when Addy turned around. "Just as lovely as a painting. Your mother won't have much work to do to make it fit perfectly."

Miss Elizabeth fumbled in an ornate silver case. "This pearl and ruby choker is what I always wore with that dress."

Addy walked closer so that she could see what Miss Elizabeth held out. Addy caught her breath. She closed her eyes and opened them again, but the choker was still there. The pearls looked so delicate next to the sparkling red jewels.

"Would you like to try it on, just to see how it looks?" Miss Elizabeth said. "You'll need to take your necklace off first. This is jewelry you wear alone."

Addy hesitated. Should she remove Uncle Solomon's protection stone? Sam had never taken it off until he'd given it to her. Addy decided it would be all right to take the necklace off just for a few minutes.

"Go on. Try it on, Addy. I think you'll look stunning," Miss Elizabeth said. "There's nothing wrong with playing dress-up."

Addy began to lift her necklace over her head, but the leather knot tangled in her hair.

"Here, Addy, let me help you," Miss Elizabeth

said, stepping behind her.

Addy felt Miss Elizabeth work the necklace free and lift it over her head. She waited for the pearl and ruby choker to be slipped around her neck. A minute passed, but nothing happened. "Miss Elizabeth, do you want me to put your choker on myself?" Addy asked, turning around.

Miss Elizabeth handed Addy the choker. She was examining Addy's necklace. "This is an interesting necklace. Where did you get it?" she asked.

"The cowrie shell belonged to my grandmother," Addy explained as she struggled with the clasp of the choker.

"No," Miss Elizabeth said. "I mean the stone. Where did you get that?"

Addy looked at the clasp to see how it opened. "From my brother," Addy said, a little embarrassed. "Some people wear those stones for protection."

Miss Elizabeth said, "You know what? I think we've played enough dress-up." She handed Addy's necklace back. "It's getting late, and I've got so much to do."

Addy stood still, not understanding. Something had upset Miss Elizabeth.

"Maybe I'll see you tomorrow," Miss Elizabeth said, her voice shaking slightly and her face flushed.

Addy gathered her old dress in her arms and walked to the door. Then she realized that she was still holding Miss Elizabeth's choker.

Addy carefully placed the choker on the bureau by the door. Then she turned and walked, as quickly as she could without stumbling or tearing the dress, down the stairs and out the back door. She squeezed Uncle Solomon's stone in her fist.

Outside, Addy felt a tear slip down her face. She clutched her own dress, leaning against the door of their new home. What had happened? Addy had somehow upset Miss Elizabeth, but she had no idea how.

Addy couldn't tell Momma about this. More tears slipped down her face. Now she was keeping two secrets. Either one of them could blow up in Addy's face.

Addy cried into her hands. Then, realizing that Momma might come looking for her any second, she dried the tears from her face. She put her necklace back on. She turned and looked at Mr. Radisson's house one last time. Then Addy took a deep breath and walked into the safety of her own house.

chapter 10

Beautiful

WHEN ADDY WALKED into the kitchen,
Poppa and Sam were eating supper.

"My word," Poppa said, "a princess done come
to our house." He called to Momma, "Come quick,
Ruth." Sam just stared at Addy as if he'd never seen
her before.

Momma rushed into the kitchen. Her hands
flew up to her mouth when she saw Addy. "You
surely right, Ben. Addy, you look like a princess in
one of those fairy stories. Lord, I wish Auntie Lula
could see you."

Addy didn't know what she looked like in the
dress. Miss Elizabeth had asked her to leave before
she got a chance to look in the mirror.

"Come on with me, Addy. Let me see where

116

those silk flowers should go," Momma said, wiping her hands on her apron. "I have two colors you can pick from."

Addy followed Momma to the sewing station in the parlor. Red and pink silk flowers were piled on a piece of cloth. "Mrs. Ford give me these spare flowers. When she give 'em to me, I figured I'd never use them. Which color do you like best?" Momma asked.

Addy quickly chose the red ones. She liked the color red. Momma told Addy to step up onto the stand. While Momma put in pins to show where she'd need to take the dress in, Addy looked in the long mirror propped against the wall. She too thought she looked nice in the dress. She wanted to feel happy. But she couldn't take her mind off Miss Elizabeth.

"What you thinking on, Addy?" Momma asked.

Addy hated telling Momma half-truths, but she wasn't ready to talk about what had happened.

Maybe it wasn't anything I did, Addy told herself. *Maybe Miss Elizabeth was just having a bad moment.* But deep down, Addy knew that wasn't true. Whatever had gone wrong had been caused by something she had done.

When Momma tucked Addy into bed after supper, she said, "I see Ida Bean is sleeping with you again. You sure you all right, Addy?"

"Yes, Momma. I'm all right," Addy said and tried to smile. But she didn't feel much like smiling. As Momma left the room, Addy hugged Ida Bean tight.

The next few days were a blur to Addy. Several times she stopped at the store for food and then put it in the basket in the shed. Twice she saw Miss Elizabeth looking at her from the porch door, but she didn't invite Addy over.

Finally it was Sunday, the day of the concert.

Miss Elizabeth had never even asked Addy how the dress looked with the silk flowers sewn on. After an early supper, the Walkers sat together in the cozy sitting room while a blustery wind blew outside. Poppa studied his spelling book, Esther played tea with Janie, and Momma was sewing.

Finally Momma put her needle down and said, "You sure are quiet, Addy. You excited about the concert?"

Addy said, "Yes, Momma." That wasn't an untruth. But Addy had a lot on her mind that had nothing to do with opera singing or a concert. Life just was never simple.

Before Momma could ask another question, Sam came home with a cherry tart for Esther. "Hey, Esther, this evening we gonna play horsy and anything else you want to play," he said, smiling as he took off his coat. "You won't even miss Momma and Addy. They gonna be so jealous."

Esther beamed, and Addy giggled despite

herself. "Yes, me and Momma, we wish we could stay home and play horsy."

Sam winked at Addy. "You better go on and get dressed, instead of minding me and Esther's business."

Addy went upstairs to wash up. She put on clean undergarments. Momma came into the room carrying the white dress. Addy hadn't seen it since Momma had finished it. It was beautiful. Momma helped Addy slip it on. "You look so pretty, Addy," Momma said. "I'm surprised Miss Elizabeth didn't come 'round to see the dress. She was so excited about it."

Suddenly it felt as if bees buzzed in Addy's stomach. So many things seemed to be happening at once, good and bad. But Addy had learned from Uncle Solomon that when something good happens and you're thinking about something bad, you've let something good get away. And bad gonna still be there waiting.

When Addy came downstairs, Poppa, Sam, and Esther all said how beautiful she looked. She sat down carefully to wait for Momma.

Finally Momma came downstairs wearing a green taffeta dress that Mrs. Ford had given her. It was a dress that some customer had not come back to pick up in three years.

"Momma," Addy said, "you look so pretty."

"My wife," Poppa said proudly. "You look as pretty as you did on our wedding days. Both of them."

Addy smiled. Momma and Poppa couldn't get married on the plantation because it wasn't legal for slaves to marry. But, like many slaves, they had had a wedding ceremony anyway. After coming to Philadelphia, they got married legally and had a real wedding in a church.

"You the prettiest woman in Philadelphia," Poppa said.

Addy's smile grew. Poppa didn't often talk like that. He was a quiet man. Momma always said,

"Poppa don't do sweet talk, he does sweet things. That's what really counts in a man, Addy."

Now Poppa said, "All right, time to go. I'll walk you to the church. I'll be waiting for you when it's over."

"We can come home all right, Ben," Momma said. "You won't know what time to come back for us."

"That's why I'm just gonna wait around outside till the concert is over." Poppa always worried something would happen at night.

Momma gave him a smile and said, "Let's go. Addy, put your coat on."

Momma held Addy's hand as they stepped out into the frosty evening and made their way to the Shiloh Baptist Church.

"It sounded just like an angel singing!" Addy said the next afternoon. Her heart beat faster as she recalled how the Black Swan's voice had soared and swooped over the hushed audience in the church. "I wish you could have heard it too, Miss Tucker."

Addy had grabbed the chance to visit the spy while Mrs. Radisson and Miss Elizabeth were out and Momma was lying down with Esther for a nap. A week had passed since Addy's last visit. She wanted to be sure the spy was all right. And for some reason, Addy wanted to tell her about the concert.

Miss Tucker listened intently as Addy talked.

"I didn't understand the Italian and German words, but it didn't matter," Addy said. "I could tell when the songs were sad or happy. Isn't that odd?"

"Not really. Human nature is the same everywhere," Miss Tucker said. "What did the Black Swan look like?"

"She didn't look anything like I pictured. With that fancy name, I thought she'd have on fancy clothes, with plumes and feathers in her hair. But she wasn't like that at all. She was very tall. She almost looked like a statue up on the stage. Have you ever been to the opera, Miss Tucker?"

"No. When I was a spy, I acted like I was a slave who couldn't read or write." She demonstrated for Addy. "Yassah, Massah. No suh, Massah."

"Why?" Addy asked.

"That way no one was suspicious of me. They didn't pay me any attention at all. Often, a group of generals would discuss battle plans while I was right there in the room."

"Was it hard to pretend you weren't smart?"

Miss Tucker looked sad for only a second. "You are a very smart girl, Addy. I hope you'll keep up your schoolwork. Education is the key to true freedom."

Addy nodded. "But was it hard for you to pretend?" she pressed, realizing that Miss Tucker rarely answered her questions.

"Tell me more about the Black Swan," Miss

Tucker said. "I've heard she has an amazing range."

"The program said she can sing twenty-seven notes," Addy replied. "From the highest note you can imagine to the lowest note a man could sing."

"You said your dress was white?" the spy asked.

Addy began to describe her dress. Miss Tucker was a very good listener.

chapter 11
A Terrible Accusation

AFTER SUPPER THE next evening, Momma used Addy for Miss Elizabeth's fitting. "I don't know what happened," Momma said, adjusting the wedding dress and pinning it as Addy turned slowly on the stand. "Mr. Radisson said she'd be over today. But she never showed up. Like she's been doing for days now, as soon as Mrs. Radisson leaves the house, Miss Elizabeth leaves."

Addy was buttoning up her own dress afterward in the sewing nook when she heard a knock on the kitchen door. Then she heard Momma inviting Mr. Radisson in.

"Where's Ben?" Addy heard him ask.

Momma said, "He's gone to the church to work on a few things. Can I help you?"

"It's really Ben I need to speak with. But while I'm here, would you show me how the dress is coming along?"

He walked into the sitting parlor with Momma. Addy had settled down on the floor to play dolls with Esther.

"Good evening, Addy, Esther, dolls," Mr. Radisson said. Then he turned to Momma. "Elizabeth hasn't said a word about the dress. I'm getting a little worried that she doesn't like it."

Momma held the dress up so that he could see it.

Addy stopped playing and looked up when she didn't hear Mr. Radisson say anything. For a minute, Addy thought he didn't like the dress.

He rubbed his forehead. "It's—it's the most beautiful dress I've ever seen, Mrs. Walker. It's stunning. Fit for a queen." He touched the white satin. "At her fittings this week, has Elizabeth said whether she likes it?"

"Sir," Momma said, looking puzzled, "Miss Elizabeth hasn't been here in over a week. On the days your mother has her ladies' meetings, Miss Elizabeth leaves shortly after. When she returns, I expect she's tuckered."

Addy could see surprise on Mr. Radisson's face. He must not have known that Miss Elizabeth went out on those days.

"I been using Addy as my model," Momma said. "But I left room for any altering I might need to do. Don't you worry none, it'll work out. And if Miss Elizabeth has a problem with the dress, we still have some time before your wedding."

Mr. Radisson excused himself quickly and left. Addy could see that he was upset.

Momma said, "I wonder what's going on with that young woman?"

Addy wondered the same thing.

...

The next day, Wednesday, everything changed—for the worse.

The minute Addy got home from school, she knew something was terribly wrong. Momma was sitting in her sewing chair, looking down at the wedding dress as if it had bitten her hands. Addy could see tears swimming in her eyes.

"What's the matter, Momma?" she asked.

"Momma crying," Esther said. "That mean lady fussed at Momma."

"What lady?" Addy asked, holding her breath. Had Miss Elizabeth finally told Momma what Addy had done to upset her?

"Esther, don't say bad things about people," Momma said, wiping her eyes with a handkerchief. "She's talking about Miss Elizabeth," Momma told Addy.

Oh no, Addy thought. "What happened?" she asked.

"I don't know what happened," Momma said.

"She came over for her fitting. She said she loved the dress. 'So lovely,' she said. I started pinning up the hem. She said Mr. Radisson told her we had run from slavery but he couldn't remember where we came from. So she asked me. I said we came from a plantation in North Carolina. I started telling her about how we got away."

"That's not bad, Momma," Addy said. "We're free now. There's no more slave catchers. I think some white people don't want to hear about slavery."

"I ain't finished, Addy. I think she was listening, but I can't be sure. I was telling her about North Carolina, and I was about to ask her to hold her arms up, when she just bolted out of here."

"Maybe she forgot something. Maybe . . ."

"She came back a few minutes ago."

Addy's throat felt tight. "What did she say?"

Esther said, "She make Momma cry."

Addy said softly, "Shush now, Esther."

Momma wiped her eyes again. Addy couldn't remember Momma ever being this upset except when they had run from the plantation and had to leave Esther behind with Auntie Lula and Uncle Solomon.

Momma sighed heavily. She stood up and laid the dress over the back of the chair. "We'll talk about this later, Addy. I best get you children some supper going."

"Momma, please tell me what's wrong," Addy said.

Momma turned around. She looked older than Auntie Lula. "Addy, I know you a good girl. You ain't never give us no trouble. It's my fault. I been putting all my time into that dress instead of watching my own children."

Addy could feel a lump in her throat as big as a potato. What had Miss Elizabeth told Momma?

"Addy, just wait until Poppa gets here. Now let me get supper on."

Addy walked outside. She walked over by the shed. Mr. Radisson's carriage pulled up at the back gate. Addy watched Mr. Radisson hop out.

She started over to ask him if he knew when Poppa would be home. Before she could catch his attention, Miss Elizabeth came running out from the porch.

Addy slipped around behind the carriage and ducked down. She didn't want to see Miss Elizabeth—not until she found out what Miss Elizabeth had told Momma.

Addy could hear Miss Elizabeth and Mr. Radisson talking loudly. They both sounded upset.

"I can't just put them out," Mr. Radisson was saying. "They have nowhere to go."

"I want them to leave," Miss Elizabeth insisted. "I think it's best for everyone's sake if they leave."

Mr. Radisson said, his voice trembling, "I told you that child saved my life. I owe them."

"It's all right, Albert. I understand. Then I'll leave. I just can't abide thieves. That girl stole my pearl and ruby choker. And I just don't think it's right for them to stay."

Addy couldn't believe what she was hearing. This couldn't be happening. Was Miss Elizabeth accusing *her* of taking the choker? Addy bet that Mrs. Radisson had put Miss Elizabeth up to this.

Mr. Radisson said, "Let me talk to the Walkers. They'll punish Addy, I'm sure. She'll return the choker and she won't do such a thing again."

Addy put a hand to her mouth. She would never steal. Momma and Poppa knew that.

"Sometimes I think your mother is right. You are too naïve," Miss Elizabeth said. "Once a thief, always a thief. First Addy stole small things—food from the kitchen, milk from the porch. Now it's my choker. There's no telling what she'll take next. And you don't know, maybe her folks put her up to it."

Mr. Radisson said, "The Walkers are decent people."

"Maybe they only act that way, Albert—so that they can gain our trust and then steal behind our backs. Your mother warned me about them." Miss Elizabeth began to cry. "Please, Albert. I won't feel safe in my own home if they're here."

Now Mr. Radisson spoke in a lowered voice. "I'm sorry. Please don't cry. Please."

Addy peeped around the corner of the carriage. She tried not to stir the horses. Her heart was bursting with pain.

Mr. Radisson hugged Miss Elizabeth and pushed the hair off her face. "Of course you must feel safe here, my dear. But let me give them some time. I can't turn them out tonight. I'll talk to Ben. I'd hate to lose him. He's the best carpenter I have."

"You can find another carpenter," Miss Elizabeth said, sniffing. "You already lost two white ones because they refuse to work beside a colored. Can't you see, Albert, just as your mother said, it might be better to have European servants?"

"They aren't servants, Elizabeth," said Mr. Radisson. "But I promise, I'll give this careful thought."

Addy couldn't stand to hear any more. She hunched down and ran to the shed. Her heart pounded louder than any drums on the earth. This was so unfair. Inside the shed, Addy sat down on the dirt floor in the darkness. She buried her face in her palms and cried. Mr. Radisson was going to make her family move, and Poppa would lose his job.

Addy's world was falling apart. But why? Addy didn't have Miss Elizabeth's choker.

Addy dried her eyes. Crying was not going to help her. She must think. Could Mr. Radisson's mother have taken the choker to make Addy look guilty? It was clear that Mrs. Radisson didn't like the Walkers.

Addy looked around the shed. Her eyes had adjusted to the dimness, and she could see the edge of the red-and-blue–trimmed basket sticking out from under the wagon parts. She suddenly realized that there was one other person who could have taken that choker—Miss Mary Tucker, the Union spy.

chapter 12

From Bad to Worse

ADDY SAT VERY still in the darkness of the shed. She wanted to trust Miss Tucker, but who else could have taken the choker? Addy thought back over her conversations with Miss Tucker and realized that she didn't really know much about the spy at all. In fact, she knew more about Miss Elizabeth than she knew about Miss Tucker.

Addy went to the shed window. Keeping her face hidden, she checked the alley to be sure that Mr. Radisson and Miss Elizabeth were gone. She waited a few more minutes. Then she slipped to the porch and sneaked inside. It was a terrible risk, but Addy had no choice. She quietly climbed down into the tunnel.

When Addy arrived at the spy's hiding place,

Miss Tucker took one look at her and said, "You better sit down. What's the matter?"

Addy sat at the table and told Miss Tucker everything. When she finished, Addy looked into Miss Tucker's eyes and asked the one question she really didn't want to ask: "Did *you* take the choker?"

Miss Tucker held Addy's gaze. "Now, why would I want a pearl and ruby choker while I'm stuck in here? Of course I didn't take it. Tell me again: What happened when you were in Miss Elizabeth's room trying on the dress? That seems to be when the problem started between the two of you."

Addy recounted it exactly as she remembered.

"Addy, a good spy must learn to use more than just her brain. Try to see the whole scene in your mind. Close your eyes. Try to remember every detail. Watch Miss Elizabeth's facial expressions. Listen to her breathing. Notice everything. Pay attention to whatever seems out of place or odd."

Miss Tucker's words reminded Addy of M'dear, Mr. Golden's mother, who had moved into the boarding house only last year. M'dear was blind, yet she could always tell when Addy was upset. M'dear had told Addy there were many ways to see.

Addy closed her eyes and thought back through the scene in the bedroom. Then it hit her. "I know. It was when she was looking at my necklace. She seemed fine up until then. She asked me who had given me the necklace."

"That was her exact question?" Miss Tucker demanded.

Addy hesitated. "I don't remember exactly."

"Hmm," Miss Tucker said. "Do you have your necklace with you?"

"Yes, right here." Addy lifted up the protection stone so that Miss Tucker could see it.

"What do you think?" Addy asked.

"Maybe she doesn't like black stones?" Miss Tucker suggested, smiling.

Addy found a giggle. "I didn't take her choker. I didn't think you would either, but I had to ask. I'm sorry."

"No harm. You did ask; you didn't accuse me. Listen," Miss Tucker said, "I think you had better go. I'll let you out." She paused a moment, then continued. "Addy, a spy often has to create or solve a riddle. This is a riddle. Treat it like one."

She accompanied Addy through the dark tunnel, said "Good luck" as she helped Addy slip out into the dusk, and then disappeared back into the passage under the floor.

When Addy got home, Poppa, Momma, and Sam were already sitting at the supper table. Food was on their plates, but it was no longer steaming.

"I called for you, Addy," Sam said.

"Where were you?" Poppa asked.

"I was in the shed," Addy fibbed.

Sam didn't say anything, but Addy saw him nod.

"Addy," Poppa said, "your momma says Miss Elizabeth claims she showed you a pearl and ruby choker. Did she?"

Now Addy wished she'd just told Momma what had happened that day. "Yes, Poppa, she did show it to me. She said I could try it on—you know, for play."

"You never told me that, Addy," Momma said. "So, did you take the choker out of her room by mistake? She is saying that it's missing. She says you took it."

"No, I didn't, Momma. Miss Elizabeth seemed upset with me, and she told me to leave. I put the choker down and left."

Sam said, "Just like that? Did you say something to get her upset?" He looked at Momma and

Poppa. "Maybe somehow Addy hurt her feelings, and that's why Miss Elizabeth is saying all this. Addy wouldn't steal."

"Hush, Sam," Poppa said. "Addy, did you have that choker in your hand?"

"Yes, Poppa. I did have it in my hand. But I put it on the bureau before I left."

"Maybe she didn't see Addy put it there," Momma suggested. "She could have knocked it off the bureau later without knowing."

"I don't know what happened," Poppa said wearily. "But Mr. Radisson says that unless Addy returns that choker, we gotta move."

Momma covered her face.

Addy felt tears slipping down her own cheeks. "I didn't steal her choker, Momma ... Poppa ... Sam. Honest."

"I ain't got no call to doubt your word, Addy," Poppa said. "But I want you to go up to your room and look around. Tomorrow I want you to check in the shed and all around the yard. Miss Elizabeth and Mrs. Radisson have convinced Mr. Radisson that you been sneaking around his property."

"Yes, Poppa," Addy said, the taste of salty tears on her lips. "I will. But I won't find it, Poppa. I don't have it."

With tears streaming down her face, Addy dragged herself up to her room. How could this be happening? Uncle Solomon's stone wasn't working at all.

Addy knew she would not find the choker, but she looked under the bed and on the dresser top and inside the dresser drawers so that she wouldn't be lying to Momma and Poppa. Then she flopped onto her feather bed. She realized that she might not be sleeping on this comfortable bed for much longer.

Where would they live? She hugged Ida Bean to her and tried not to cry.

Finally Addy whispered to Ida Bean, "I have to become a spy now. Miss Tucker helped save the Union. I have to help save my family."

Addy fell asleep wondering why this was happening to her family. Hadn't they been through enough?

In the middle of the night, Addy sat straight up in the bed. Esther was coughing hard. Addy threw back the covers and hopped out of bed. She knelt beside Esther's bed. She rubbed Esther's forehead until she stopped coughing. Addy said, "I want you to have good dreams, little sister."

When Addy went down to the kitchen the next morning, Momma was cooking oatmeal. "Soon as you eat, Addy, I want you to go out and look for that choker."

Addy said, "Yes, ma'am. But I won't find it, because I didn't take it, Momma."

A knock sounded on the door. Addy and Momma both looked up in surprise.

Momma opened the door.

Mr. Radisson was standing outside. His face was grim. "Good morning, Mrs. Walker. Is Ben here?"

"Yes, sir," Momma said. "Come in. I'll get him."

Poppa walked into the kitchen. "Sir, I thought you didn't want me to work today? I'll get my tools."

"No," Mr. Radisson said. "As I said before, this matter needs to be resolved before you can return to work. To do that, I must ask Addy a question."

"Go ahead, sir." Poppa looked puzzled.

Mr. Radisson said, "Addy, is it true that you go into the shed almost every day?"

Addy stammered, "Yes, sir."

"I was the one who told Addy she could go in the shed," Momma said. "She likes to play in there."

Mr. Radisson pursed his lips. He sighed heavily,

his shoulders drooping. "I'm sorry to say this, but I found Elizabeth's pearl and ruby choker hidden in an old trunk in the shed."

Momma let out a small cry. Poppa put his hand on her shoulder. "I'll handle this, Mr. Radisson," he said.

Mr. Radisson shook his head slowly. "No. I'm afraid I have to let you go, Ben. You have one week to find a place for your family to live. I am so sorry."

He turned toward the door and then came back. "I'm afraid I need to take the dress, Mrs. Walker. Of course I'll pay you what I owe you for your work."

Momma went to her sewing corner, where the dress was hanging on a hook. She took it down and gave it to Mr. Radisson. "You don't owe me nothing, sir. We sorry for the trouble."

Mr. Radisson nodded his head and left.

Momma sat at the kitchen table. Poppa lowered his head and walked out.

"Momma," Addy said, "I did not steal her choker. Someone else must have hidden it in that shed. But it wasn't me. Honest, Momma."

"Addy, I want to believe you," Momma said. "But if you didn't take it, then who did?"

"I don't know," Addy replied, wondering if Miss Tucker had told her the truth. The spy could have taken the choker and hidden it in the shed. *But if Miss Tucker did that,* Addy told herself, *wouldn't she have hidden the choker in the false-bottomed basket?* Then Addy had another thought—that suspicion is an ugly thing.

At supper the Walkers ate in silence. Addy had never seen her family so sad. She wondered if they all believed that she was a thief.

After supper, Sam pulled Addy aside. He said, "Addy, I know you didn't steal anything, but think, how could that choker have gotten into the shed?"

Addy shook her head. "I don't know." She wanted to tell Sam about the spy. But she couldn't. She wasn't a thief—and she wasn't a traitor, either.

Addy went to her room and sat down on the floor with Ida Bean to think. Miss Tucker had said that a spy either creates or solves a riddle. Addy tried to imagine how a spy would handle this riddle.

Miss Tucker had said Addy should try to remember everything—every detail. Suddenly Addy recalled the conversation she had overheard by the carriage yesterday between Mr. Radisson and Miss Elizabeth.

Had Mrs. Radisson put Miss Elizabeth up to this? It didn't seem to Addy that Miss Elizabeth would behave this way on her own. After all, Miss Elizabeth didn't mind Negro servants. She'd even told Addy that she didn't understand why white people would allow coloreds to cook their food but not sit down and eat with them. *And*

Miss Elizabeth knew all about the Black Swan, Addy thought, *and she didn't mind having tea with me and Momma. She even gave me her favorite dress.* It didn't make any sense. Why would she try to get rid of Addy's family?

Addy needed to find out more about Miss Elizabeth if she was to solve this riddle. Momma had said that on the mornings that Mrs. Radisson went out to her ladies' club, Miss Elizabeth would leave, too.

Addy made up her mind. Tomorrow morning, if Miss Elizabeth left, Addy would be right behind her.

chapter 13
The Riddle Deepens

ADDY DIDN'T GET much sleep that night. Thoughts buzzed in her mind. And Esther's cough was getting worse. Three times Addy got up to comfort her through violent coughing spells.

On Friday morning, Addy helped Momma get breakfast ready and then acted as if she were going off to school.

Instead, Addy hid in the shed. The morning was gray and chill. Soon, rain mixed with snow began to spatter the shed window.

Eventually, a carriage came to the back gate for Mrs. Radisson. Shortly after, Addy spotted Miss Elizabeth hurrying toward the back gate, an umbrella held over her head and a dark rain bonnet shielding her face.

Addy watched Miss Elizabeth walk out the gate. Then Addy followed her, staying far enough behind that Miss Elizabeth wouldn't see her if she turned around.

It was raining hard now. Addy wished she had a rain cape. After a few blocks, Addy began to wonder where Miss Elizabeth could be going. She walked a long way, keeping to the alleys. Addy wondered why she hadn't gotten a carriage. Addy's feet felt frozen, and she was soaked to the bone. Her legs began to hurt. But she'd walked longer escaping slavery.

Now she was in an area where the alleys were strewn with garbage, doors hung lopsided off their hinges, and men stood huddled together on the corners. Addy looked up at the street signs and saw that Miss Elizabeth was approaching Gillis Alley, near Lombard and South Streets. Suddenly she knew where she was: in the worst part of the Seventh Ward.

Addy had never been to this part of Philadelphia. Here, people looked almost as poor as they
had in slavery on the plantations. Poppa would not
want Addy here by herself. Addy glanced around.
Miss Elizabeth was the only white person she'd
seen for blocks. Everyone was colored. Why on
earth would Miss Elizabeth be coming here?

Squinting against the rain, Addy watched Miss
Elizabeth hurry into one of the shoddiest-looking
row houses on the block. Addy waited until Miss
Elizabeth had disappeared inside before she
walked closer. Everything about the house was
dirty: the door, the wooden trim, the windows.
Some of the windowpanes were broken and covered with newspaper. There were holes in the walls
where bricks had fallen out. Addy read a small
sign on the door. It said *Idey Station House.* Addy
knew that people who had no place to live often
ended up at a station house.

Addy realized she couldn't feel her feet. She

needed to warm up—and besides, she wasn't going to find out much just standing outside.

Addy crept inside the building. The hall was dark and silent. She ducked under the stairs, waiting to see which apartment Miss Elizabeth was visiting. She tried not to breathe in the smells of cooking grease and rotten food.

Finally, a door opened down the hall and Miss Elizabeth stepped out. An old colored woman stood in the doorway. Addy watched as Miss Elizabeth hugged the old woman and pressed money into her hand, then turned and walked slowly out of the building. Addy stayed hidden for a few more minutes. Then she went over to the apartment door and looked at it. The number nine was on it. Addy turned and left.

Outside, she spotted a bearded colored man putting a wad of tobacco into his mouth. He was leaning against the building. He didn't seem to mind the cold or the rain.

"Sir, excuse me," Addy said, "but do you know the people who live in this building?"

"Some of 'em," he said.

"What about the lady in number nine?" Addy asked.

"I don't reckon I knows her, but she like the rest of us. Come off a plantation down South."

Addy was surprised. "You're sure she's not from Connecticut?"

"Ain't sure. But don't know nobody 'round here that weren't just out of slavery. The Freedmen's Society done helped everybody in this station house come here. I don't reckon no plantations in Connecticut to come from."

Addy said thank you and walked away. He was right, of course—there were no plantations in Connecticut. So how would Miss Elizabeth know somebody in this building? Then Addy remembered Miss Elizabeth saying that she was taking her old dresses to some charity people. Maybe the charity had sent Miss Elizabeth here—but she hadn't brought a dress with her to give away. Addy had only seen her give the old woman money.

It wasn't the first time Addy had seen somebody mean act nice. She thought of Master Stevens. Sometimes he had acted as if he really liked the slaves who worked in his house. But Poppa had told Addy that Master Stevens didn't truly like them— he just cared about them same as he liked his old hounds. Maybe to Miss Elizabeth, this old colored lady was like a pet.

Addy shuddered and headed home.

By Friday night, a river of bad news had flowed into the Walker house. Esther was getting worse. Poppa hadn't found a job. Even Mr. Miles Roberts, Poppa's old boss, didn't have work for him. Momma couldn't find any sewing jobs. And Poppa wasn't having any luck finding a place for them to live.

Time was running out, and Addy was no closer to figuring out what was going on than she had been the day Miss Elizabeth had accused her of stealing the pearl and ruby choker. She'd missed a day of school to follow Miss Elizabeth, and even that hadn't helped. Now Addy wondered if her own family would end up in the Seventh Ward.

There was only one thing left for her to do.

chapter 14

Caught

ON SATURDAY MORNING, Addy kept
watch on Mr. Radisson's house from her window
until she saw Mr. Radisson, his mother, and Miss
Elizabeth head off in a carriage. Addy took that as
a sign that today was the day.

Addy was alone downstairs. Sam was at work,
Poppa was out looking for a place for them to live,
and Momma was upstairs tending Esther, who
was feverish and coughing. Addy slipped out of
the house and crossed the yard to Mr. Radisson's
porch. She let herself into the kitchen.

She walked catlike across the flowered carpet
of the dining room to the massive stairway that led
upstairs. The house seemed scarier without anyone
in it. Even though the day was bright outside, the

house was dark and dreary. Two statues of men stood in the hall as if to guard it.

As Addy walked up the stairs, the eyes on the large portraits on the wall appeared to follow her. At the landing, Addy stopped. A part of her wanted to run back downstairs. But she had to find out more about Miss Elizabeth. And the only way to do that was to search in her room.

Addy had thought about telling Miss Tucker that she was going into the house, but she had decided against it. Addy still had a nagging feeling that Miss Tucker might have had something to do with the missing choker.

Addy moved along the upstairs hallway until she reached Miss Elizabeth's bedroom. She paused in the doorway and studied the room. Where should she start? What was she looking for? She didn't know.

Addy walked to the dresser. She tugged at the top right drawer. But then, on the dresser top, she

spotted the ornate silver case that had held the
choker. Addy opened it. Inside was the pearl and
ruby choker she had supposedly stolen. Her heart
speeded up.

Addy pulled open a few of the drawers but
saw nothing unusual. She felt funny seeing Miss
Elizabeth's personal things, so she tried to work
faster.

Suddenly Addy felt chilled. What if Mrs.
Radisson or Miss Elizabeth caught her here? She
had to hurry and get out. Addy stood against the
dresser and scanned the room. Under the window,
she noticed the leather trunk engraved with Miss
Elizabeth's initials.

Addy opened the trunk. She felt as if the room
were spinning. Addy lifted a familiar-looking quilt
out of the trunk. She unfolded it and spread it out
on the bed.

Amazing—there were Auntie Lula's special
patterns: The star in the upper right corner, with

the moon just under it. In the opposite corner, a man looking to the left and a woman beside him looking to the right. There in the center, a tree with the branches growing out to each side opposite each other. And down in the bottom corner—Uncle Solomon's mark.

Addy touched the quilt with her fingers, tracing every appliqué. It was so much like her own quilt, the one that she had had to leave behind on the plantation. Was it her old quilt? No, Addy could see that it wasn't. She could see some differences in the pieces of cloth that had been used to make the designs.

Addy knew it was time for her to get out. The last thing she needed was to be caught in Miss Elizabeth's room. Addy folded up the quilt. She was about to set it back into the trunk, but something forced her to look a little further. Addy shoved aside a few small items and picked up a crumpled piece of silk.

Something fell from the silk and landed on the floor with a soft thud. Addy reached down and picked it up. It seemed to be a handkerchief tied around something small and heavy. Addy was about to untie the knot when she heard footsteps on the stairway and the sound of someone humming.

Panic raced through her. Addy stuck the handkerchief into her pocket. She hurried to put the quilt back the way she'd found it. She scurried under the bed. Peeping out, she saw a corner of the quilt hanging outside the trunk. Addy squirmed out from under the bed. She threw open the lid of the trunk. She had to put the quilt back exactly as it had been.

But it was too late. Miss Elizabeth stood in the doorway.

Addy froze. She couldn't even breathe.

"What are you doing in here, Addy?" Miss Elizabeth screamed. She grabbed Addy's arm and pulled her into the hallway.

Mrs. Radisson appeared from a nearby room. "What on earth is happening?" she demanded, her eyes flashing anger as she caught sight of Addy.

"I found the Walker girl in my room," Miss Elizabeth said. She pulled Addy through the house, Mrs. Radisson following close behind. As they went out into the backyard, Miss Elizabeth shouted, "Mrs. Walker!"

Momma ran to the door. "What is going on out here?" she asked.

"I caught her red-handed," Miss Elizabeth said. "In my room."

"I told you she was a thief!" Mrs. Radisson hissed.

Momma looked as if someone had just slapped her in the face. "Please let her go," Momma said. "I'll take care of her."

Addy was crying now. She had never seen Momma so upset. Addy knew she shouldn't have gone into the Radissons' house. She shouldn't have gone through Miss Elizabeth's things. "I'm sorry, Momma, honest," Addy pleaded. "I wasn't trying to steal."

Momma pried Addy's wrist from Miss Elizabeth's grip. "I will deal with Addy," Momma said.

"That's what you and your husband said before," Mrs. Radisson replied. "I want you people out of here. Tonight. Not tomorrow—*tonight.* Do you hear me?"

Miss Elizabeth said sharply, "Yes, I think she's right. Tonight!"

"I heard you," Momma said. "We'll leave." Momma pulled Addy by the wrist back into the house.

Mrs. Radisson stood with her feet apart and shouted, "You're lucky I don't fetch the police!"

Momma slammed the door shut and leaned against it for a moment, her face in her hands. Then she looked up and said, "Addy, Esther is real sick.

I gotta take care of her right now."

Momma walked from the room and headed up the stairs. Addy followed behind her.

Up in their room, Esther was lying in bed, beaded with sweat. "Momma," Addy whispered. "What's the matter with her?"

"I don't know. As soon as your Poppa come home, I want him to find a doctor."

Momma began bathing Esther's forehead with a damp cloth. "She's hot as fire. She's talking out of her head, Addy. Go fetch some more water."

Addy ran to get water, pulling her coat off as she hurried into the kitchen. She heard something fall from her coat onto the floor, but she didn't have time to pick it up. She reached for a pitcher and darted back upstairs to give Momma the water.

In a tiny voice, Esther said, "Auntie Lula, I'm hungry."

Addy felt tears sting her eyes. Every breath

Esther took was a painful wheeze. How could everything be going so wrong?

Momma lifted Esther into her arms and rocked her, humming softly. "Addy, go fix you something to eat," Momma whispered. "Ain't no use you getting sick too."

Addy went back to the kitchen. She didn't know what to do with herself. She looked aimlessly around the silent room. She noticed Miss Elizabeth's knotted handkerchief on the floor and realized that that's what had dropped from her coat earlier.

She picked it up. She knew she shouldn't have taken it from Miss Elizabeth's trunk. She wished she could give it back. Addy fingered the cloth and laid it on the table. Then she untied the handkerchief.

Addy stared at the object that lay inside. She picked it up. Her fingers trembled as she held it to the light. It was a black protection stone.

Addy turned it over. She saw the mark—the very same mark—that Uncle Solomon had carved on her own protection stone. Addy dropped the stone as if it were a burning coal.

She felt around her neck. Her stone was there. She picked up the other stone. She removed her necklace and compared the two stones, laying them on the table side by side.

They were the same.

"Addyyyyyy!"

At the sound of Momma's scream, Addy ran upstairs to her side. "Oh, Momma," Addy whispered, seeing Esther's limp body.

"Addy, your sister is dying. Go get help! Quick!"

Addy did the only thing she could think of. She ran to Mr. Radisson's porch. She shoved the table aside and yanked the rug up. She raced down the steps, sliding and falling to the bottom. She picked herself up and stumbled through the darkness. She climbed the last flight of stairs yelling, "Miss Tucker, come quick. Help!"

Miss Tucker said, "What on earth?"

Addy could barely catch her breath to speak. "My sister's dying. Please help."

Miss Tucker snatched up a lantern and her carpetbag. They both raced from the hiding place out onto the porch, across the yard, and into the house.

Addy said, "Momma, I think she can help."

Miss Tucker didn't bother to tell Momma who she was. "What are the child's symptoms?" she asked, taking Esther from Momma's arms and laying her down on the bed. "Bring the lantern closer," Miss Tucker said.

Momma brought her the lantern. "Are you a nurse? A doctor?" Momma asked.

"I'm a friend of your daughter's. How long has

the little one been this way?" Miss Tucker asked, gently lifting each of Esther's eyelids.

"A few minutes," Momma said.

"Good. Quick, Addy, go into the house and get some ice. Shave some off, and hurry."

Addy took off. She went onto Mr. Radisson's porch without caring if anyone heard her inside. Addy was about to go in the kitchen door when she was stopped.

Mrs. Radisson stood in the doorway. "Where do you think you're going?"

Behind her, Addy heard someone say her name. She turned to see Miss Elizabeth coming up out of the secret passageway. "Addy, you knew there was a squatter in this house!" Miss Elizabeth said, waving the secret note the spy had written. "Your name is on this paper as big as day."

Mrs. Radisson said, "I'll have my son fetch the police on the lot of you."

"Ice—my sister—she's dying. She needs ice.

Please," Addy said, crying and holding out her hand. "Please."

Miss Elizabeth's face changed. She dropped the paper to the floor and said, "Follow me."

Mrs. Radisson said, "You'll do no such thing." She stood in the doorway, blocking their entrance.

Miss Elizabeth pushed past her. "Go on home, Addy. I'll bring it."

Addy hesitated. But then she ran. She got back to her room, breathless. "Miss Elizabeth is bringing the ice."

Miss Tucker had opened her carpetbag and taken out her smelling salts. She held them to Esther's nose, but Esther didn't stir. Momma moaned softly.

Miss Tucker stood up. She shook her head. "I'm sorry. I know how to mend wounds, but I don't know how to do anything for her. I'll go fetch a doctor, but I fear it may be too late."

Miss Elizabeth stepped forward, past Miss Tucker and Momma. She set down a bowl of ice chunks and held her hand to Esther's forehead. She pressed her ear to Esther's heart. "Mrs. Walker, go to the kitchen and find me some mustard seed, oatmeal, and vinegar. You, Addy—go upstairs to my room. Look in the trunk, at the very bottom, and bring me the brown leather sack. *Quick.*"

Addy moved like lightning.

Inside the big house, Mrs. Radisson reached out and grabbed Addy's arm as Addy raced up the stairs. "You aren't to go back up there."

Addy pulled her arm free, leaving Mrs. Radisson holding air. Mrs. Radisson screamed something after her, but Addy couldn't hear her.

She took the stairs four at a time. She almost fell going into Miss Elizabeth's room. She threw open the top of the trunk, tossing out everything until she spotted the leather sack. She grabbed it and flew home so fast, she wasn't sure her feet touched the ground. Addy handed the sack to Miss Elizabeth.

Miss Elizabeth fished several small bags and bunches of strong-smelling herbs and roots from the sack. She asked for boiling water, a bowl, scissors, and clean cloths.

Momma, Addy, and Miss Tucker got everything Miss Elizabeth wanted. Then they stood back, barely breathing, holding on to each other.

Addy didn't know how time moved forward. As she stood there watching, she couldn't even remember what time was, or if time had ever existed. All she knew was that nothing was more important than her little sister's life.

Addy prayed, but she did not bargain with God. Uncle Solomon had told her that was fool's talk. "What could you have to offer God?" he said to Addy once when she vowed she would do anything for God if He would only let them escape slavery. Now, Addy hoped that God, too, wanted Esther to live.

Momma squeezed Addy's hand.

Esther made a sound like a trapped kitten. It was one of the sweetest sounds Addy had ever heard in her eleven years of life. Then she heard Esther say in a whisper, "Momma."

Momma hurried to the bed. "Can I pick her up?"

"Not yet. Just comfort her," Miss Elizabeth said. "Don't take the poultice off her chest. And keep putting hot water in the bowl and holding it up to her nose." Miss Elizabeth stood up to go. She wiped her face with the hem of her blouse.

Miss Tucker extended her hand. "Thank you."

Miss Elizabeth stepped back. "Who are you?"

Addy said, "She's my friend."

Miss Elizabeth studied the spy, her eyes narrowed. "You are the person who's been squatting in Mr. Radisson's house. Mrs. Radisson is going to have you arrested."

"No," Addy shouted. "She can't do that."

"Just because I helped your sister doesn't

mean anything has changed," Miss Elizabeth said to Addy.

Suddenly, Addy could see fear in Miss Elizabeth's face. And, in that moment, things took on a new shape. Addy could see what had been there all along. Every clue.

chapter 15

The Tale Is Told

ADDY LOOKED INTO Miss Elizabeth's eyes. "I think I know who took your choker," she said.

Miss Elizabeth stared back. "You should know, since *you* stole it," she replied finally.

"No," Addy said. "You stole your own choker. Didn't you?"

Miss Elizabeth flushed. "What are you saying? Why on earth would I steal my own choker? You're making no sense at all."

"For a long time, I couldn't understand what I did to get you upset, back when I was trying on your dress," Addy said. "But now I see that it didn't have anything to do with me. It was the stone that upset you—Uncle Solomon's protection stone."

174

"What a silly thing to say! Why would I care what kind of stone you have?"

"Wait," Addy said. She hurried down to the kitchen, snatched the two stones from the table, and went back.

"See these?" Addy said, displaying the stones on her palm. "They match. They have the same markings. Both of these stones came from Uncle Solomon. One of these stones is mine. And the other one I found in your trunk, Miss Elizabeth, tied up in a handkerchief."

Momma was sitting close beside Esther, one hand on the sleeping child's chest. In a whisper she said, "Let me see those stones, Addy." Momma held the two stones up. "They do match. Together they make one of the designs on Auntie Lula's quilts. How on earth...?"

"And Momma," Addy said, "Miss Elizabeth has a quilt just like the one Auntie Lula gave me when we was on the plantation."

Momma turned to Miss Elizabeth. "I don't understand. Lula never made but three quilts. Addy had one, Solomon's sister had one, and Lula and Solomon had one. How did you get these things?"

"I don't know what she's talking about," Miss Elizabeth said, her voice shaking.

"That's not all, Miss Elizabeth," Addy went on. "I heard the song you were humming when you caught me in your room. I didn't recognize it at first. But just a minute ago, the song came back to my mind. See, Miss Elizabeth, I know that song."

"So what if you do?" Miss Elizabeth looked away. "Lots of people know lots of songs."

"Not this song," Addy said. "This song Uncle Solomon made up himself."

"All this is nonsense! What does any of this have to do with the theft of my choker?" Miss Elizabeth took a deep, shaking breath. "I want you all out, and that squatter is going to jail."

Miss Tucker said quietly, "You're doing fine, Addy. Now just think: What happened once Miss Elizabeth convinced Mr. Radisson that you'd taken the choker? Sometimes you have to look at the results to understand why a person did something."

Addy thought back. The result of Miss Elizabeth's accusation was that Mr. Radisson had fired Poppa and told the Walkers to leave. Why would Miss Elizabeth want that to happen?

Addy bit her lip. She knew most of the pieces of this riddle. There was only one part she hadn't figured out: Miss Elizabeth's visit to the Seventh Ward. Did that have anything to do with the riddle? Or had Miss Elizabeth only gone there to do charity work?

"I'm going home," Miss Elizabeth said. "If you all know what's good for you, you'll leave. Now. Just leave, and I'll see that Mrs. Radisson doesn't call the police on you."

"Don't threaten Addy—she's just an innocent child," Miss Tucker said quietly. "But I'll leave."

Addy's eyes flew to the spy. "No! It would be dangerous for you to leave. Please don't leave." Addy turned back to Miss Elizabeth. "I don't understand—you seemed so nice at first. And you must have been a good person once, if Uncle Solomon gave you the stone."

Addy saw Miss Elizabeth flinch at her words. *Uncle Solomon.* A piece of the puzzle fell into place. "I think I know why you accused me of stealing your choker," Addy said slowly. "You *wanted* Mr. Radisson to turn us out of this house—because you were afraid that I'd figure out you used to know Uncle Solomon. But... but why would you care if I knew?" Addy was thinking out loud now. Her heart was beating rapidly.

Uncle Solomon. Suddenly Addy caught her breath. "Uncle Solomon lived in North Carolina his whole life. He never left the plantation until just before he died. He sure had never been to Connecticut. And—and that means you aren't really from Connecticut either, Miss Elizabeth. You're from the South. That's how you know the old slave woman in the Seventh Ward."

Miss Elizabeth looked as if all the blood had drained from her body. "How do you know about her?"

"I followed you. An old man there told me that all the people in the building were straight off plantations. So that means"—Addy's thoughts raced—"you had relatives who were slave owners? No, there has to be more to it than that. Maybe . . . maybe . . ." Suddenly Addy knew. "You owned slaves. You were a slave owner, Miss Elizabeth. Weren't you?"

"Addy, be careful what you saying," Momma warned.

But Miss Tucker nodded encouragingly. "I think you've found the answer to the riddle, Addy." The spy turned to Miss Elizabeth. "She's right, isn't she? You knew that if Albert Radisson found out you had once owned slaves, he would refuse to marry you. I don't know him, but I knew his uncle. Frank was a decent and courageous man. He understood how slavery damages the human soul. His nephew would never marry a slave holder, not even a reformed one."

Miss Elizabeth began to sob. "It's not true. None of it. You have it all wrong." She buried her face in her hands.

Addy thought, *Maybe she truly is sorry for holding slaves.* But something was still out of place.

Addy closed her eyes. The image of Miss Elizabeth setting the poultice on Esther's chest stirred in her mind. Miss Elizabeth had done exactly what Uncle Solomon and Auntie Lula would have done. But how could Miss Elizabeth know their healing art? Uncle Solomon and Auntie Lula would never have taught it to a slave holder. Never.

Addy almost stopped breathing as the answer to the riddle became clear.

Addy needed to check one last thing to be sure that she was right. She walked over and picked up the leather sack she'd taken from Miss Elizabeth's trunk. Uncle Solomon had always carried a brown leather healing sack. Addy turned the sack over and looked at the bottom.

There was his mark.

Uncle Solomon would no more have made one of his sacks for a slave owner than he would have given his soul to the devil.

Addy raised her head. In a clear voice, she said, "You ain't white, Miss Elizabeth. That's it, isn't it? You are a colored woman."

"What are you saying, Addy?" Momma breathed.

"Oh my," Miss Tucker said. "Is that it, Elizabeth?"

Miss Elizabeth sank onto a chair. She looked

down at her hands. "It all started out so simple," she said finally, almost whispering. "Then it got more and more complicated. I met a man and fell in love. There was only one problem. He was white. And I—I was just pretending to be white."

For a moment, the room was silent. "How did you know Solomon?" Momma asked finally.

Miss Elizabeth's brown eyes glittered with tears. "I'm his sister's child—his niece. My real name is Bessie."

Momma shook her head.

"I grew up on the Carter plantation, right next to Mr. Stevens's plantation. When I turned sixteen, I escaped, leaving my poor mother behind. Her name was Matty. She was a healer, just like Uncle Solomon. When I was little, Uncle Solomon helped to raise me. He and my mother taught me the healing arts." Miss Elizabeth's voice trembled, and she paused a moment to steady herself.

"In Connecticut, Quakers helped me go to

school. But when I graduated, I couldn't find a decent job. Then one day I walked into a shop and they thought I was white. They hired me on the spot. As time went on, I got better and better jobs—but only because people thought I was white." She lifted her head and looked at them. "Who was I hurting? I had no family left. And then I met Albert Radisson. There seemed no reason to tell him the truth. I could move to Philadelphia and start a new life with him, a good life."

Addy stared at Miss Elizabeth, struggling to understand what it would mean for a colored person to somehow live as a white person. Addy thought of the policeman who had stopped her family on their way to Society Hill. She thought of Poppa's work crew refusing to work with him just because he was colored. In a way, Addy could understand Miss Elizabeth's choice. And yet Addy's heart was aching with pain. She touched her necklace and felt the comfort of her grandmother's cowrie shell and

Uncle Solomon's stone. What about the part of Miss Elizabeth's life that she had left behind?

"The woman in the station house," Addy said softly. "Was that your momma?"

"No, Addy," Miss Elizabeth said through tears. "That woman took care of my mother on the plantation until she died. She's the one who saved the quilt for me. When I lived in Connecticut, I sent her money. Now I take her the money and make sure she has food."

Miss Elizabeth looked at each of them in turn, her eyes pleading. "I'm so sorry for what I've done to you all. I felt desperate, especially after meeting Albert's mother. It was obvious that if she knew I was colored, she would never consent to our marriage. I couldn't let her find out the truth.

"You know, Addy, at first I really couldn't find my choker. When Mrs. Radisson suggested that you had taken it, I just went along with her. It was a terrible thing to do. But once it started,

I didn't know how to stop it."

Addy shook her head. "Poppa was gonna lose his job, and people thought I was a thief."

"I'm so sorry, Addy," Miss Elizabeth said. "Please forgive me. I—I will tell Albert the truth—about everything. I don't know whether he will marry me once he knows what I've done. But I promise you, I will see to it that he knows you and your family have done nothing wrong."

Miss Elizabeth turned and started toward the door.

Momma reached out and put a hand on Miss Elizabeth's arm. "You caused us a lot of trouble, ma'am," she said. Then she looked down at Esther, sleeping peacefully at her side. "But you saved my baby's life today."

For a moment, Miss Elizabeth's eyes rested on Esther. Then she quietly left the room.

• • •

Late that evening, Poppa came through the door, letting a blast of cold air into the kitchen. The rest of the family was there waiting for him. Addy and Sam were washing the supper dishes while Momma sat at the table with Esther asleep in her arms.

Momma looked up. "Did you talk to Mr. Radisson, Ben?" she asked.

A smile broke out on Poppa's face. "I have good news," he told his family. "We don't have to leave, and I got my job back. Mr. Radisson wants you all to know he's sorry 'bout everything."

"Oh, thank goodness," Momma breathed.

Addy felt like jumping with happiness, but there was something else she wanted to know. "What about Miss Elizabeth, Poppa?" Addy asked. "Will Mr. Radisson still marry her?"

"I don't know what they'll decide, honey," Poppa answered gently. "They have a lot to think about."

Somehow, Addy couldn't help hoping. She knew that Miss Elizabeth had done some terrible things, but she also knew that Miss Elizabeth loved Mr. Radisson. If things were fair, Addy thought, color would not matter and Miss Elizabeth wouldn't have been trying to pretend to be white.

"What about Miss Tucker?" Addy asked.

"Mr. Radisson is allowing her to stay in the house for now," Poppa answered. "He's working with friends of his uncle to make sure it'll be safe for her to start a new life soon."

"The Lord makes a way," Momma said.

Poppa bent down and put his arms around Momma and Esther. Sam went over to join them.

Addy ran to her family and hugged them all. At last, they were all together and safe in their new home.

Inside Addy's World

The period just after the Civil War was a time of hope for black people. For the first time, former slaves—more than four million in all—could live and work where they wished, learn to read, marry legally, and own property. Families like Addy's began building new lives in freedom.

Black people had long struggled to end slavery. Once the war began, tens of thousands enlisted as Union soldiers. Others supported the Union just as bravely, but in secret—as spies.

The most famous black spy was Harriet Tubman. Best known for helping slaves escape on the Underground Railroad, during the war she operated a highly effective spy network in South Carolina. Another daring spy was Mary Elizabeth Bowser, a former slave with a photographic memory. Pretending to be uneducated, she became a servant in the Confederate White House, where she listened to President Jefferson Davis's conversations and read his letters. The information she provided to the Union was so crucial, and her position in Davis's home so dangerous, that she is now included in the U.S. Army's Military Intelligence Corps Hall of Fame.

After the war, Bowser kept the story of her spying secret. Like other black spies, she feared harm from

Confederates angry about the South's defeat. Indeed, the war nearly destroyed the South. By war's end, its cities were in shambles, and many farms were ruined or abandoned.

The U.S. government poured money into *Reconstruction*, the rebuilding of the South. The goal was to heal not only the war's devastation, but also slavery's terrible injustices. Schools for newly freed people opened. A constitutional amendment gave black men the right to vote, and sixteen black men were elected to Congress.

But Reconstruction soured fast. Southern states passed laws called *Black Codes* to limit black people's freedom. They could be fined or jailed for leaving their plantation, not working for a white person, or forming a black church without police permission. In the North, blacks had a harder time finding jobs and were paid less than whites. The prejudice that Addy experiences was all too common.

To escape these troubles, some light-skinned blacks "passed" as white. But their freedom from prejudice came at a high cost: the constant fear of discovery. Worse, to pass successfully, people had to cut all ties with relatives and old friends, or visit them in secret. Many who had passed before they married never told their spouse or children, so that later generations never knew of their black heritage.

Read more of ADDY'S stories,
available from booksellers and at *americangirl.com*

⊙ *Classics* ⊙
Addy's classic series, now in two volumes:

Volume 1:
Finding Freedom
In the midst of the Civil War, Addy and her mother risk everything to mak a daring escape to freedom in the North.

Volume 2:
A Heart Full of Hope
As Addy and Momma make a new life in Philadelphia, they find that freedom brings new chances—and has great costs.

⊙ *Journey in Time* ⊙
Travel back in time—and spend a day with Addy!

A New Beginning
Discover what Addy's life was like. Outrun a slave catcher, raise money for soldiers, and help Addy find her family. Choose your own path through this multiple-ending story.

⊙ *Mysteries* ⊙
Enjoy more thrilling adventures with BeForever characters.

The Jazzman's Trumpet: A Kit Mystery
A valuable trumpet is missing, and Kit must prove *she's* not the thief.

The Smuggler's Secrets: A Caroline Mystery
Is Caroline's uncle selling precious supplies to the enemy?

The Puzzle of the Paper Daughter: A Julie Mystery
A note written in Chinese leads Julie on a search for a long-lost doll.

A Growing Suspicion: A Rebecca Mystery
Who is jinxing the Japanese garden where Rebecca volunteers?

A Sneak Peek at

A New Beginning

My Journey with Addy

Meet Addy and take an exciting journey into a
book that lets *you* decide what happens.

After dinner, Grandpa pulls out his old coin collection. He's got a story to tell about every single coin. I think I've heard all of them about a million times.

"Look, Sweetpea!" Grandpa snaps open a small plastic case and holds up a coin that's not silver and not gold. I lean closer. This is one I haven't seen before.

"This is a bronze two-cent piece from way back in 1864," he says.

"Wow! That's a million years ago!" my little brother, Danny, shouts.

"Closer to a hundred fifty," I say, doing the math quickly in my head.

"That's right," Grandpa nods. "My father had an uncle, Charley Long, who fought in the Civil War. Uncle Charley saved this coin and passed it down to my father, who passed it down to me. Someday I'll pass it on to you." Grandpa is looking right at me. It's clear that this coin means a lot to him.

Grandpa sits back on the sofa and examines the two-cent piece. "This coin was part of your great-great-granduncle Charley's first pay after he became a soldier," Grandpa explains. "He sent his money home to his parents, and his mother kept this one coin all during the war—she carried it with her every day. It reminded her that one day the war would end, and she hoped with all her strength that her son, Charley, would come home safely."

Grandpa's story gives me goose bumps. Ever since my dad took a job out of town and my mom went back to school full-time, I hardly ever see them. There's nothing like a war keeping our family apart, but I can't help thinking that I miss my parents just as much as great-great-granduncle Charley must have missed his.

Later, when I'm in my room changing into my PJs, I hear Danny making some commotion in the hallway. I open my door to check it out.

He's dragging part of Grandpa's coin collection into his room! "Hey!" I whisper. "Give me that, or you'll be in big trouble!" I try to grab the box away from Danny, but he yanks it out of my reach. Then he drops it. Plastic sleeves and cases fall out. We both scramble to pick them up, hoping Grandpa hasn't heard us.

"I only wanted to get a closer look," Danny says. "Don't tell!"

"All right, I won't," I agree, closing Grandpa's coin box. "Now go get your jammies on."

As I take the box into my room, I step on something. It's the plastic case holding the two-cent coin from great-great-granduncle Charley. It must have landed in my room when Danny dropped everything. I pick it up, snap open the case, and examine the coin more closely. Grandpa usually polishes his coins, but this one has some dirt crusting over the date stamp. I use my thumbnail to rub the numbers *1864*. My fingers start to tingle, and I feel dizzy. I close my eyes for a second and shiver from a gust of cold air. When I open my eyes, I can't quite believe what I see.

I'm still holding the coin, but I'm not in my room anymore. Instead, I'm outside, on a pier, standing next to an enormous ship. Somehow my PJs have been replaced by a faded dress. I've also got on thin wool stockings, black lace-up boots, a scratchy shawl, and a bonnet with frayed ribbons tied under my chin. Another gust of wind sweeps over me, and I shiver again. It's cold, and whatever I'm wearing isn't nearly warm enough. Where did these clothes come from? Where am I?

Wherever I am, there are boats—and people— everywhere. The ships docked along the water-front seem really old-fashioned—they're all made of wood and have giant sails. Workers scurry to steady huge crates that swing from ropes overhead as they're unloaded from the ships.

A steady stream of people starts leaving one of the ships. Most of the women are well dressed in long, full skirts and fancy bonnets, and the men wear suits with long coats and tall black hats. Some carry cloth bags, while others give directions to crew members struggling with large trunks. A few people from the boat walk onto the pier carrying nothing but small bundles. Their clothes look as thin and worn as mine. These travelers are all African American, and they stand in a small group next to a stack of crates. Some are as old as my grandparents, and there are children in the group, too. They all seem unsure of what to do next.

I notice a horse-drawn wagon stopping at the end of the pier. I can't help staring. *Horses?* I look up and down the street, realizing that I don't see any cars. I don't see anything modern. Now I don't just wonder where I am—I wonder what year it is.

An older African American man in a suit climbs down from the front of the wagon, and several people hop off the back of the open bed. The man motions my way—is he waving at me? I duck behind the crates, not sure I want to talk to anyone. Peeking around the crates, I see a girl about my age standing next to the man from the wagon. She's wearing a blue dress and a faded shawl, but her smile is bright and friendly. The group from the ship starts to move toward the wagon. Suddenly the people from the ship and the people from the wagon are shaking hands and hugging one another as though they're long-lost friends.

I'm curious about the people on the pier and the girl by the wagon. I step out from my hiding spot and start to navigate my way through the crowd. I'm almost at the wagon when I bump into a man wearing one of those tall black hats. He glares at me as if I've just insulted him.

"Watch where you're going, colored girl!" he yells. The tone of his voice makes me jump. He's really angry with me. "You people should remember to keep your place!" he adds before rushing away.

My heart is racing. Jeepers, it was just an accident! I don't understand why he had to be so fierce. Why did he call me "colored"? Isn't that a not-very-nice word for black people? And what did he mean by "keep your place"? Don't I have just as much right to be here as anyone else?

I look around to see if anyone saw what happened, but no one stops or even seems to notice me. Through the crowd, I see the girl. She's wrapping a blanket around the shoulders of a thin woman who is sitting in the back of the wagon. When she turns, the girl catches my eye and smiles. "Hello," she shouts over the hustle and bustle around us. "Welcome to Philadelphia!"

Philadelphia? So that's where I am. Isn't it known as the City of Brotherly Love? Someone forgot to explain that to the man in the tall hat.

I approach the wagon. "My name's Addy

Walker," the girl says. "Welcome to freedom!"

"Freedom?" I repeat. I'm confused.

"Yes!" Addy says, taking both my hands.
"You're not a slave no more!"

But I never was a slave, I say to myself. I think
of Grandpa's coins and his Civil War stories. When
the Civil War was over, slavery was over too.
Grandpa told us that lots of people escaped that
horrible life before the war ended, though. Did
great-great-granduncle Charley's coin transport me
to Philadelphia during the Civil War?

Author's Note

Thanks to Connie Porter for creating such a memorable character, and kudos to Vertamae Grosvenor for acknowledging the service of Mary Elizabeth Bowser.

Thanks also to all the scholars who've written invaluable resource books, beginning with W. E. B. DuBois and including so many others that it is impossible to list them all. My story could not have evolved, however, without the meeting of fact and fiction in the writing of Lorene Cary and Frank J. Webb, the exposition of Wendy Ann Gaudin, and the scholarly interpretations of Edward L. Ayers and William Cohen. I give much respect to magazines and Internet sites such as *Boston* magazine, historyworld.com, and eyewitnesstohistory.com.

To Matt DeJulio, administrator, Society Hill Civic Association; the Historical Society of Pennsylvania; and those who preserve historic houses and buildings everywhere—my hat is off to you.

And thanks to the Philadelphia real estate agent who knows so much about historical homes. Bravo!

About the Author

EVELYN COLEMAN grew up in
North Carolina with her parents and
brother, surrounded by a large extended
family. Today, she lives in Atlanta, Georgia,
with her husband and enjoys spending
time with her two grandchildren.
She has written many award-winning
books for children and young adults.